Albert McConachie's Bad Day & Other Tales

Rex Mangin

Published by Rex Mangin – 2023
Revised - 2026

Contact the author at: rex.mangin@xtra.co.nz

Also available as an e-book

Cover Design: Alexandra Taylor

ISBN 978-0-473-66436-7

Books By Rex Mangin

Available as paperback and e-book

Infidelity Gun Running &
    Other Tales

Cold War Warrior

Flying The Pacific

Mercenary

Albert McConachie's Bad Day

Carrie Gray

Travel Bites

Contents

Foreword

The mundane, trivial, amusing, domestic, and the downright catastrophic. Everyday events, childhood memories. With a little bit of imagination you can probably relate to these happenings. A collection of short stories that will entertain and amuse. There are a couple of true stories included as well.

The tale about Albert McConachie is in three parts, softened by some intervening short stories.

Albert McConachie's Bad Day

It starts early, Albert's still in bed half asleep, he can hear her shuffling along the hall. Why does she have to shuffle, why can't she lift her feet. It's deliberate, intended to let him know that she's up doing things, and he's not. *'Get up, it's late.'* It's said in a quiet 'combative' voice, trying to wind him up, spoil his day, punish him. She can be like that in the mornings, why? No reason, it's just the way she is. A bad start, pisses him off. Whatever happened to *'upsy dear, breakfast's ready, your favourite, eggs benny.'* No, nothing like that. She's been up for a while shuffling about, making just enough noise to let him know she's up, making herself useful while he's lazing in bed, happens every morning. The only way Albert can defend himself is to leap out of bed when she does. Strike first, be full of enthusiasm, start making the breakfast. Next it will be a grumble about some imagined slight, sour breakfast, kill any small talk. She's just in a bad mood first thing in the mornings, must be in the genome, a female thing. Are all females like this? Albert doesn't know, he's never lived with another woman. Could ask around, get real, what will people think. *'Marriage over Albert, all turning to custard is it?'*

Bathroom, shower, whiskers off, not a very cheerful image in the mirror. Get into a better frame of mind, *try harder*, can't just be pissed off. Why would she want to ruin his day? Does it give her a sense of power, get him on the ropes, a hard left right first thing, punishment, for what? What is it he's done to cop this? Does she love me, used to, what's gone wrong? I bust my guts for her, try really hard, do all the right things, take her out, spend all the money, expensive holidays abroad, put in a lot of extra time at the office improving my position, climbing the salary ladder, slave around the house, the maintenance, the big garden. *'Get up, it's getting late.'* Well get over it Albert, it's not that it's something new in your life, well actually it is, never used to be like this. Once, a while ago now when he thinks about it, she was loving, affectionate, considerate, but all that seems to have morphed into something quite different, not nice at all, why?

Breakfast, small talk, well Albert is mouthing some words but they are falling on barren ground, she's ignoring him, winding him up some more, perhaps there's some sort of a psychiatric problem, must be. One small pleasure, dog, the little creature loves Albert, always makes a big fuss, especially at breakfast, it's a Bichon, a little fluff ball, a rug rat, something nice in his life. *'Coffee dear,'* he makes an effort, no response, he tries again, she grunts, unintelligible, *'I said coffee!'* *'yes'* she snaps, *'can't you hear.'* Oh dear this is worse than the usual morning disaster, great start. Just clear out, go to work, bust my guts all day, for what, come home to this poisonous atmosphere, life just has to be better than this. *'I may be a bit late home'* he ventures, spur of the moment thought, he's not going to be late, but it might fetch a response, it doesn't. *'Bye dog, I'm off.'* Albert's parting shot, not exactly a peacemaker but what the hell, she's just being the complete bitch, where is my life going?

Suddenly; the distinctive sound of tortured tyres tearing at the pavement, *Albert's tyres!* Wait for it, the inevitable crunch, no, made it, just. There's nothing between Albert's car and the one in front, no gap at all, but no crunch. His right leg has cramped up with the sudden tension, it's hurting, he jerks it straight, heel down, toes up, push down hard, usually works. The dick-head in the car in front, what was he thinking. The lights had just changed from green to amber, 'the accelerate light,' well around here that's what amber means. There were a couple of cars in front of him. They did not slow down, that's the way it is in traffic. 'We'll just race through on the amber' but the driver in front of Albert must have been having a bad day as well, an apparent increase in speed, a moment of indecision, enough time for Albert to start accelerating, suddenly bright red right in front, *right in front, STOP!*

Albert's heart is thumping, really thumping, his leg is hurting and suddenly he does not feel well. He has stopped, just, there's some tooting from behind, typical. The lights run through their sequence, turn green, the idiot in front disappears, not a thought in the world about the near mayhem he has caused. Albert's still stopped, does not feel well. Some loud tooting, snap out of it, you're blocking the intersection, get going!

He makes it into the company car park. Albert's risen through the ranks sufficiently to warrant his own space, it's a godsend. Traffic, parking, public transport, it's a nightmare, a private spot in the carpark, priceless. He sits there, immobilised, not feeling well, thinking, my life is crap, why? Self-pity, no time for that, life is what you make it, and heaven knows I certainly try. Perhaps I can make this day work for me, put in a big effort, turn things around, take some flowers home. That would be a surprise, could lighten things up, improve the atmosphere, yes it is a good idea. I'll make a serious effort today, tail up, go for it.

Albert sits for a while thinking about his new resolve, his new initiative, his 'about to be better life' when his current life intrudes. I'm going to be late, bugger, that's a big no no around here. He leaps out of the car, races across the car park, up the stairs and his leg, his sore leg, cramps up, crash. He's sprawled on the stairs, the concrete stairs, his trousers are torn, there's blood. Don't be late, they're restructuring, everyone is being assessed, even talk about redundancies and re-applying for your current position. Albert is quite convinced his star is rising, he certainly puts in a lot of time, has a company car park, he's next in line for the section manager position, his job should be secure, don't blow it all. There is competition, that young Neville thinks he's a rising star, bit of a 'greaser' young Neville. Into the office, *he is late*, dishevelled and bleeding, great. Has he been noticed? *the whole office has noticed*. Is there any understanding, sympathy, compassion, this is my 'new start' day.

There is some sympathy, Adele is very sympathetic, that's nice. Helpful, understanding, she's a looker as well, lovely personality, why have I not got an Adele at home? Well actually I did once but somewhere along the line she changed, why? I don't know. Should I make a play for Adele, change my life dramatically, start afresh. Dream on, have you seen Adele's man? There's always Cathy, the office 'cow,' she's available, she's always available, couldn't miss there. Forget it Albert, come back to your world, the real world, this is your 'new start' day remember.

It's an average day at the office for Albert, one of many average days, no good work stories. Well there was one, his arrival, but that was not something he wished to remember. Adele had been very good, helped to clean him up, plaster on the knee, even found a pair of trousers.

'*The lovely Adele fixed me up with a smart pair of trousers when she saw the mess my own had become.*' That will go down well at the pub, not so sure about home.

The end of Albert's 'new start' day, '*what about a beer or two at the pub?*' It was Robert, he was a good guy, a mate. So far there had been no signs of a new start for Albert but he was optimistic, the day was not over.

'*Adele, what about a drink, Robert and myself are going to drop by the pub for a couple.*'

'*Love to.*'

It was several beers and it was nearing seven when they called it quits. Albert had said he would be a little late.

Driving home and would you believe a booze bus, damn, how many did I have. Albert was worried, my 'new day.' I had struck up a closer relationship with Adele, but now this.

'Evening sir, have you been drinking?'

'Yes officer I've had a couple.'

'What's your name and address sir?'

'That's a positive for alcohol, would you pull over here please.' The usual breathalyzer, Albert is sweating.

'That's ok sir, you're just under.

'Thank you officer.'

Home, damn, the flowers? Oh well it's not as if I had promised. I'll try a kiss and a cuddle, might work; wrong!

She was parked on the sofa in front of the TV watching some mind numbing nonsense, did not respond to Albert's effort at a cheery greeting.

'Sorry I'm a bit late dear, I did mention it this morning.'

'It's in the oven,' was the only response.

A burnt offering, she could have made some effort, but no. It'll be separate bedrooms next. Could it be the name, McConachie? Albert's older sister reckoned it was cursed, something from the dark ages. She did the unthinkable and changed her name to 'Conchie.' The ultimate insult, disowning your family name. Didn't work, she's still a spinster. But then she was never blessed in the good looks department either, poor girl. Don't see much of her now, went right off at a tangent when she did the name change thing, reckoned she had to distance herself from all things McConachie, pity, I was quite fond of her. She moved away, a long way away, well clear of the McConachies.

What to do, Albert eats the burnt offering alone in the kitchen with the dog.

'That was lovely dear, ' absolutely no response, how much of this can I take, there could be a breaking point.

12 Albert's Bad Day

Imagine Adele on the sofa, scantily dressed, inviting, an erotic film on TV. There's got to be some pleasure in life, even Cathy would be better than this. What to do? right now I think I'll just go to bed, the little dog will be my mate, it's everybody's mate. Tomorrow? a repeat of today? there's got to be a better life.

'You've been drinking, you stink of beer.'

The words were venomous, she spat them out, why, oh why, is my life so terrible.

I Need To Go Back

The new millennium. I'm in my mature years reflecting on life, it's something that just happens along with a little forgetfulness and a feeling of mortality, *mortality*, scary stuff!

That time so long ago. Germany during the Cold War. I was very young. What happened then made an indelible impression on my mind. I was a pilot on a nuclear strike squadron. Had the Cold War heated up I was going to wreck nuclear devastation on Eastern Europe. Hard to comprehend after all these years. Was I really going to do that? I was all of twenty something at the time and yes I was going to do it.

I've never been back, not met up with my old squadron mates. Nostalgia is setting in, *I need to go back*, I need to meet my colleagues from that time, that incredible, unbelievable time. Did all that really happen? Yes it did, and when I think about it, it's frightening. I guess I'm lucky to be here, to have survived. Had the war started I would not have seen day two. They called it MAD, mutually assured destruction, it would certainly have been that, but the war did not start, some dangerously close calls, but no war. Now here I am in my mature years tucked away in the South Seas. It's where I was born, a wonderful place, a place where I will see out what years I have left. *I need to go back*, I need to see my old mates, and I need to do it sooner rather than later.

The idea just came to me, no reason. With the passing of time it got stronger, *I need to go back*.

The Internet, that extraordinary medium. A couple of hours and I was able to make contact. We have to get together, time marches on, my mortality is very much in mind. It happened. I made contact with a squadron mate from that time long ago. A Kiwi who lived in

England, married an English girl, made a career in the Royal Air Force. He still had contacts and being a good organiser, he always was, he arranged a get together of the people from Germany, the ones he was able to track down. It got better, the old squadron, now a high tech fighter outfit flying the latest jets, was having an anniversary, an open day at their airfield. Flying displays, a 'dining in' for squadron members, an insight into the latest simulators, fighter aircraft, and much more. We were invited to be the squadron's guests on this special day. My mate managed to track down ten others from the old squadron, a reunion was organised to coincide with this anniversary.

A trip to England, a long way, need to fill it out, make it worthwhile. For me just meeting up with my compatriots from those Cold War years was sufficient but I was taking my partner of many years along. She was keen to visit some distant relatives in Ireland and some friends in England so we stretched it out to four weeks. A bit of Hong Kong shopping on the way, always gets a girl's attention.

It's a long way squeezed into a small seat, well the budget version is a small seat and it was a budget version. Good movies though, managed five first runs I think, made the time pass.

London, been a long time, seemed much the same, fascinating place. Met up with friends from home who were off on a cruise, we did some touristy things together. The pubs were the highlight, they're great in London, memories came flooding back. Then there was the pub food, well yes, I think we're a bit spoilt in our part of the world. Our New Zealand friends went off on their cruise, we headed north, a week in the countryside with our English friends. The reunion was some days off and our hosts wanted to show us 'everything English.' They did a grand job, Ely Cathedral, some Newark Horse Studs, numerous fine pubs and restaurants, historical spots, several places where Oliver Cromwell featured including his house, a thoroughly enjoyable few days.

Then off to the small village where our reunion was going to take place. We'd booked a local hotel for the get together. It was next to the RAF Station where the old squadron is now based with their state of the art jets, the place where the anniversary celebrations were going to take place, it was a moving experience. It had been forty-five years since I had seen these fellows. The highlight for me was reuniting with my navigator from that time, my poor suffering navigator. The terrors I had subjected him too hurtling around the northern part of Germany at high speed just as low as we could go. We had been part of a low level strike outfit and did a lot of low flying. He had aged, we all had, forty-five years is a long time, it's just that the picture in my mind was of a young chap.

We downed many beers and told tall tales, there was a lot of 'do you remember,' nostalgia was thick in the air. I had a lump in my throat, why had we left it so long? No reason, it's just that time marches on and we tend to be so busy with our lives that there's not time to reflect, until suddenly, well in my case it happened suddenly, you become aware of your mortality and you start to reflect on your life.

There were a couple of fellows who could not make the reunion, poor health, we were all in our seventies, lucky to still be here. Someone had the phone contacts and after many beers there was some phone calling. This moistened the eyes, it was incredible just to hear their voices. There was a meal, a really good meal, the hotel made a big effort for our group, more drinks, more reminiscing.

We were welcomed onto the airfield the following day by the current CO and well looked after, squadron members from yesteryear. I had never thought about that, suddenly I felt seriously old, am I old? We were split into two groups, each assigned a current squadron pilot. We scored a young lad in a flying suit, they were all young lads. This keen young fellow appeared to be very young but when you think it through that's exactly what we must have looked like all those years ago. We ribbed him about whether he was only allowed out of school to fly his hot jet at the weekends. There was a flying display, it blew me away. One of the current squadron jets, the things it could do, made the vintage jets we had used to defend the West look very ordinary. Then we were shown a modern jet simulator, small, very high tech, I was impressed. I was even more impressed when I was invited to 'have a go.' Our 'schoolboy' guide then took us to a hanger where we were allowed to get into the cockpit of one of the squadron's current aircraft. So different, there was little I could actually relate to. I found myself engulfed in a great wave of nostalgia, oh to be young again. There was a lot of picture taking in front of these modern fighter aircraft.

That evening we again enjoyed a long session in the bar and an excellent meal in the hotel. We had elected to have our own 'dining in' at the hotel, just us 'elderly fellows' from Germany, we thought it would be more enjoyable, it was; it was also the last time I was to see my old navigator.

Next morning we dispersed far and wide. My partner and I went over to Cork in Ireland and enjoyed a week on an Irish dairy farm, different, very different. Coming from New Zealand it was a revelation to see how the Irish did it. We travelled around the southern part of Ireland, it was so enjoyable, I was introduced to Murphy's, a fine drop indeed. Back to London, onto the big jet, little seat again, more first run movies, a shopping stopover in Hong Kong then home, and terrible news.

I received an e-mail from my old navigator's son in England, my compatriot from the Cold War years, the person I had shared so many experiences with. He was undergoing surgery on a knee and had unexpectedly died under the anaesthetic. It put a real damper on everything. I contemplated flying back to England for his funeral but that was just not practical. I got onto my mate in England, well I now had several newfound mates, and made sure that the old squadron was represented at Harry's funeral. I wrote a eulogy and got another squadron mate to deliver it at the funeral service.

It was a couple of weeks later that the son contacted me again to tell me how much these things were appreciated. The eulogy from yesteryear, from the far side of the world was a highlight.

So I've been back. It's now a year or two since that trip, I'm even older, even more reflective. Perhaps I should make it all happen again; sooner rather than later.

The Christmas Sewer

'Santa's here,' small children wildly excited, 'a limo! Santa's got a limo!'

'Santa!'

Santa climbs out of his limo, big bag on his back, looks promising, they crowd around, little faces full of expectation.

It's our turn, the children's Christmas party, it's a big one, lots of children, should be plain sailing, I think everything's covered, what did we miss? Relax, enjoy the moment, have some fun with the kids, this will be a lovely day, you'll enjoy it.

That's in a perfect world; hard to find the perfect world.

'Rex, there's a murky looking puddle and a bit of a smell in your drive, noticed it when I was Ho Ho Ho'ing down there, better have a look.'

'Geez Santa, thanks, is that my prezzy?'

It'll be that b----y sewer, great timing, how many kids are there, twenty, thirty?

'Sorry no toilet.'

'Get real, there's got to be a toilet!'

'Fix it.'

Yeah right, just go out there and fix it.

'Do you have any idea what's involved dear?'

'Well forget it then, we've got this party to deal with, fix it later.'

'Ah later could, will, be a disaster.'

'Well don't bother with it now, we're very busy; would you get those chairs up from the garage and -------- '

'Yes dear.'

It was a marvel of modern engineering in its time, the clay tile drain. How can a tile be a drain, a tile's flat. Trees of the world rejoice, man has just created an everlasting food source for us all. Every house, every building, anywhere man habitates, a sewer, a permanent meal, an easy one, just wiggle on in and feed.

We built the house some time ago, state of the art, drains, make sure you get the drains right, don't want trouble there. All done according to best practice, everything worked as advertised, for a while! It was a mid year Christmas, you know that trendy practice that occupies those winter evenings during the deepest darkest part of winter; your turn this year.

'Rex, there's a puddle in your drive, bit of a smell too, noticed it when I pulled into your drive.'

'Is there? I'll have a look in the morning.'

The puddle was a lake in the morning, a lake of sewage, the most revolting sight imaginable and the smell, what had our party guests been eating? No matter, it was all in the drive, never made it to the sewage farm. Sunday, a call to the emergency drain unblocker, get a bank loan, and the problem goes away, but it sure spoilt Sunday, and the smell, will the neighbours comment?

Three years on, our turn, mid year Christmas again.

'Rex, there's a puddle in your drive, bit of a smell too, noticed it when I pulled into your drive.'

Not again, we had it fixed last time, how come it's reoccurred? Like rust, trees keep growing. It's pelting down, can it wait till morning? It had better, not enough cash in the house, or the ATM, to get it fixed right now.

Another horrendous bill, need to give this problem some serious thought. The Christmas sewer, that's what it is, a lovely present when we host a Christmas party. It's not going to happen at our place again, ever!

A bit of research. An investment in a set of rods, you know, the ones that wealthy drain unblockers use, would be money well spent. Down to the trade supplier. There's a knowledgeable chap there who knows about these things, an hour later I'm an expert. Another bank advance, and I become the owner of a full set of professional rods. Ok sewer, just pull that trick again, but it didn't, not for a long while, I forgot about it.

The mess was streaming down the drive from a gulley trap right up by the house, stinking grey liquid with bits of white stuff, the sewer had awoken. It was a mid week morning, I had a bit of time off and I had those rods, those rods! Where are they? Relief, under some gear at the back of the garage. It was an interesting day. I had not realized just what a revolting business it is, no wonder they want all your money. Plenty of Dettol, you can catch things from sewage and there sure was plenty of that, the smell, something you never forget, the moment those man hole covers come off, yuk!

So I'm a practiced drain unblocker these days, just don't want to have to utilise my skills. There's a pattern, about every third year the tree roots need dealing to. Plan ahead, get in first while the sewage is still flowing, and do the storm water at the same time. Yes, good thinking; the reality, 'oh s--t it's the sewer,' been about three years, why didn't I remember.

'Look dear this sewer thing has to be dealt with now, you'll have to hold the fort for a couple of hours and try to keep them out of the toilet.'

'What do you mean a couple of hours, I need you to do the BBQ, then there are the drinks, you can't just disappear.'

'Please try to understand dear, please! This is serious, if I don't fix it now, all these kids are going to create a big mess, a huge mess, in the drive.'

'Well why didn't you do it before the party.'

Good question, why hadn't I? the recurring three year problem, remember, yes I remember, have you ever forgotten something? Some things you're just not allowed to forget, they will bite you on the bum if you do.

'Well it's not good enough.'

'No dear, sorry.'

The Kiwi Pie

Flakes of pastry spill down my shirt, the good flaky stuff, an essential part of a decent pie, steak and cheese, my favourite.

I'm enjoying a Kiwi institution, a meat pie and it's from one of the best in the business, the local pie shop. He's got it sussed, makes the greatest pies around. There are others, pretenders to the throne, but the local pie shop reigns supreme, been there since forever, the pies never vary, consistency, absolutely essential.

You can't get them beyond our shores, the world is missing out on a real taste thrill, well I think so.

The pastry, the key ingredient, must be light and flaky, then there's the filling, it's here the pie maker can showcase his skills. The options are endless. I'm a bit conservative, invariably steak and cheese, always perfect at the local pie shop, quality steak, never a trace of gristle. I've been enjoying his pies for years, keep suggesting he enters the pie competitions, would have to be a winner, I know, I'm a connoisseur. I've tried many of the winning pies around the country, they're all good, yes indeed, but the local lad, I reckon he's on the money.

How is it a small bit of pastry, stuffed with whatever, can get a Kiwi so excited? Is it addiction? probably, brought up on the things. That craving for a meat pie, it can be very strong. When I was a lad, a long time ago, I found myself in London with a strong desire for a pie, a small meat pie, there must be a pie shop somewhere? Nope, they don't have them, tough! I did find a pie, but it was a big one, it was alright, well the little bit I ate was alright, but the pastry was not really flaky and I found a bit of gristle. Nostalgia had me close to tears; it was a cold wet London day as well.

You bite into a pie, the pastry flakes off down your shirt front, you could use a knife and fork but holding it in your hands and burning your lips adds to the taste thrill. The flavour, yum, the gravy has to be just right, usually is, most pie shops are pretty good. Competition is keen, the standard high, one dud pie will condemn the purveyor to the 'don't go there list' forever. The small size is just right too. The queue outside a good pie shop testifies to their popularity.

Once upon a time there was a chain of pie shops in New Zealand, Georgie Pie, they sold very good pies for a dollar, a real bargain, incredibly popular. Then an offshore fast food outfit came along, bought them up and closed them down, competition. A New Zealand icon was removed from the scene, very unpopular move.

After years of agitation the villain of the piece agreed to re-introduce the Georgie Pie and sell it at their numerous food outlets. Great excitement, Georgie Pie is back. Nostalgia of course had caused the old Georgie Pie to morph into the most magnificent of pies that would leave the opposition far behind. Expectation was high, the pie shops were on notice. The great day arrived, total disaster, the 'new' Georgie Pie was awful. The pastry, the essential part, was not flaky, not flaky, how can you have a pie that does not have flaky pastry? Well the new Georgie Pie had a rather leathery type of pastry, what was even worse, it was more expensive than the far superior offering from the local pie shop.

Pity really, the pie eaters of New Zealand had been expecting a return to the good old days of cheap, very good pies. Were they really that good? or was it nostalgia?

The Supermarket pie, there are a lot of them, frozen, and there lies a major point of difference. A pie must be fresh, once it's frozen it loses a lot, believe me, I know these things, I'm a connoisseur, remember! Reheat, must, absolutely must, be done in an oven, a microwave will ruin any respectable flaky pastry, makes it soft and mushy, might as well settle for a ham sandwich.

24 The Kiwi Pie

Whenever a trip down country is on, the planning takes in the known good pie shops, there are quite a few including award winning ones. The return trip is arranged to allow for the purchase of a few of the better ones along with the Pokeno bacon and the Mercer cheese. There's some good stuff south of the Bombays!

Peckish? I'll just duck up to the village and get a couple of pies, ok? Yep, good idea, 'Mexicana for me.'

'One Steak and cheese, one Mexicana please, you should enter the competitions, you'd be a winner, believe me.'

'Oh no no could not do that.' He's very shy our local pie shop man, comes from East Asia and he makes pies to die for. The sign outside his shop says it all, 'buy one or we'll both starve.' I like that, he's a good chap, could do with a few more like him.

Home with the pies, plate, knife and fork perhaps, they're pretty hot, 'no I'll use my hands.' Bad call, the steak one is really hot. I bite into it, flakes of pastry spill down my front, and ouch, I burn my lips, perhaps a knife and fork is a good idea. The taste is divine, the texture of the pastry, the chunks of tender steak, the rich gravy, I'm in heaven, again. Every time it's the same, a unique taste thrill and it appears it's confined to our part of the world; aren't we so lucky.

Tomato sauce, it's a fact of life here, very popular, Australian gravy, and some people just have to drown everything with it. A meat pie, something to be savoured, a sensation for the taste buds, one of life's finer things; appreciated for its unique flavour, the tenderness of the meat, the richness of the gravy, the texture of the pastry, and some cretins have to smother the whole thing with tomato sauce.

I'm sure tomato sauce has its place on this planet, it's very tasty and does indeed compliment some dishes, but on a meat pie, criminal!

The Cottage

It's the nicest house on The Parade, we know because passers-by keep telling us. An address - The Parade - that bit of expensive real estate on one of Auckland's best beaches, the million dollar houses, and our little cottage sitting in the prime spot. The nicest house on The Parade.

Big double glazed ranchsliders opening onto a veranda, a veranda from yesteryear, a rarity. Tin roof, balustrading, filigree and finials, cane chairs and big cushions. Everything white, whiter than white, looks, great but its greatest asset, the view, a big panoramic view. Right on a beach, good swimming, all tides, just across the road. The long flat road that's frequented by the health brigade, cyclists, runners, joggers, strollers, dog walkers, a lot of dog walkers, everyone around here has a dog, a dog they just have to walk every morning. Beyond the beach a busy harbour estuary. Lots of boats, everything, ferries, tugs, big yachts, small yachts, launches, gin palaces, tinnies, jet skiers, paddle boarders, wind surfers, kite surfers, foiling kite surfers, that's really exciting. The list is endless. Oh yes the very latest, wing foilers. All so fascinating, just sit on the veranda and be entertained.

It was not like this a short while ago, oh no, definitely not!

It started with a drive along the beachfront.

'Look dear it's for sale.'

'What's for sale?'

It was a dunga, a real dunga, a dilapidated old wreck, a bach from years ago, seventy plus years ago. Peeling paint, weeds growing up the walls, mould, broken windows, overgrown garden, well not a garden just a surrounding wilderness.

'We have to have it, my mother always said she would just love to live in that lovely little house.'
Curse the day mother ever laid eyes on it. My life was about to change; dramatically!

An auction.

'We must go, I *want* that house.'

'It's *not* a house dear.'
An obsession, how in h--l can we afford it, prime real estate on one of the city's most desirable beaches.

'W*e have to have it.*'

'Yes dear,' anything for peace.
It will pass, tomorrow the wild enthusiasm will have died, wrong, the desire just got stronger.

'We'll sell our house, it must be worth a lot of money.'
Our lovely big house in suburbia, all the creature comforts, big garden, manicured lawn, mature trees, birds, recently modernized, ultra modern kitchen, the envy of our friends, and you want to trade it for a dump on the beach. Mind you the dump was on prime real estate, freehold, a very desirable spot, but a dump.

'We'll do it up, you like doing things like that dear.'

'Really, I never knew that, and at my stage of life. Do it ups are for young people not mature pensioners.'

'We'll get bro on the job, he's good at auctions, bit of a hobby.'
Bugger she really is serious. We had thought about downsizing, this could be it, don't miss the moment, it won't come around again, a cottage on the beach, her lifetime dream, she really is serious, this could be a life changer.

It was tiny; little rooms, three very little rooms, and little doors, lots of little doors, they built funny houses in the 1930s, must have been little people, I don't recall Dad being little!

Auction day, our lives could change here. She'd been right onto it, given it her all, sorted out agents, auctioneers, briefed bro, our bidder, it was serious stuff, I just stood there gobsmacked. 'Yes dear,' where is this leading?

It was an outdoor affair, big crowd, mostly locals stickybeaking, *what will the cottage fetch?* Not many serious buyers. We had done our homework, valued our lovely house, figured what we could go to.

'Welcome ladies and gentlemen.'

He was off, painting a picture with words, blah, blah, blah. The dunga apparently was the greatest real estate opportunity of the century never to be repeated. Paradise on the beach, where else are you going to get a piece of prime beachfront freehold, this 'character cottage' was a fantastic opportunity. Rubbish, it was a dunga, a broken down wreck that had never been maintained, fit for the knacker's yard!

There were a couple of cautious 'low ball' bids, some people are ever hopeful, then a serious one, someone wanted the dunga. *I was in a daze, not quite there, what are we doing.* I recall gazing up at the roof and wondering about the kikuyu grass growing out the top of a downpipe.

Bidding slowed, there was just one other, and bro! The 'other' was keen, kept pushing it, bro showed his expertise and burned him off. Suddenly it was over, we now owned the thing, the dunga, cracked windows, corroded hinges, peeling paint, kikuyu all through it, *what the h--l have we done?*

The money, where's the money coming from. We had just paid top dollar for this 'slice of paradise.' The real estate market was booming, booming all right, we had just been 'boomed.' Our house, our lovely house, another auction, another top dollar affair, just as well!

'Dear we have to move out; now!'

'Surely not the dunga, we can't live in that, need to rent something.'

'Have you seen the going rate 'round here, that's if you can find anything.'

'It's the dunga then.'

'Afraid so, could be interesting.' It was.

Character building is the expression, do I need more character? We managed to squeeze the essentials into the dunga, the rest of our stuff, and there was a lot of it, into storage, need to be some serious decluttering, and soon. Most of the windows were cracked, hinges had no movement, there were numerous holes that the south-westerly howled through, cold, miserable, what have we done? I forced a window, have to be able to open something. The hinges were corroded solid, the only movement was what the corroded hinge screws allowed in their rotted holes. 'Crack,' the window glass shattered, I was close to tears. *Ritz to the pits*, how appropriate. We'd hit rock bottom, things can only get better. There was one nice touch, the ancient toilet had a soft close seat, cut above the crappy last minute paint job.

Suddenly we became motivated, seriously motivated. There was a flurry of activity, the place was totally gutted, a whole new cottage arose from the dunga's bones. There were extensions, verandas, re-piling, double glazing, insulation, a modern kitchen, landscaping, new garaging, it went on and on and through all this we lived onsite, that was interesting, and challenging. Here we are to-day, the envy of our friends, well worth all the hassle.

'Just one small thing dear, no more driving around looking at old houses.'

Be A Good Lad And Get The Bread

Bread, man's basic food, been around since the dawn of time, it'll still be around on the fateful day when we get it all wrong and blow ourselves up.

'Be a good lad and get the bread.'

'Ok Mum.'

A morning ritual. I hop on my bike and pedal down to the bread shop, it's not far, the early morning bike ride is refreshing, very refreshing during the winter.

'White or wholemeal?'

'White please.'

It's still warm, just out of the oven, tempting. Pedalling home I pull a piece of delicious soft warm dough from the open face of the loaf, yum, another piece perhaps?

'That's naughty, I've told you before, I need this to make the sandwiches, now there's only half a loaf.'

'Sorry Mum, won't happen again.'

It's too tempting, I do this every time, can't help myself. Always the white loaf, wholemeal's yuk! Only two choices, white or wholemeal. That was yesteryear.

They call it white flour now, then there's wholegrain, cape seed, multigrain, high fibre, Turkish, ciabatta, focaccia, mixed grain, and yes, wholemeal.

'Sandwich or toast cut sir?' It's a whole new world out there in breadland.

Remember those days? I'm sure I was not the only kid who got the bread in the morning, had to take lunch to school, sandwiches. There was a tuck shop that sold meat pies, real yummy, but you needed money.

I love bread, I'm a bread nut. We have excellent bread here. Competitive business, bakeries everywhere, one man operations, franchises, overseas chains, the supermarkets are into it and the Asians, they are right into it. All good news for the consumer, keeps the standard right up there.

'Man cannot live on bread alone,' someone said that once, but I'm sure man could last for quite a while, especially on our bread. What is it about the stuff, it's only flour and water. It's all in the making, great skills are required, try it. You have? You've got a bread maker in a cupboard somewhere, everybody has one. We bought them a few years back, remember? We were all going to make fabulous bread, and we did, we convinced ourselves. It was great bread, all those recipes, all those little extras, the special flour, must be Australian, it's better, excuse me, something Australian is better? 'Ah, yes, their flour is better for bread making,' hhmm, bit hard to take but I will admit there's a smidgen of truth to that. When all the furore died down we went back to the bakery, their bread was really good, we were not even in the ballpark! The bread maker went back in the cupboard where it's remained. So ended the great bread-making era. Can't even get rid of it on Trade Me.

A couple of years ago I came across an American Airline hostess buying a lot of a popular full grain wholemeal bread in a supermarket here, bit different! A bread nut like me, she too had discovered that the bread here is pretty good. She was taking some, a lot actually, home with her, you've got to be keen! She was!

Back to yesteryear, a time when we were not blessed with too many bakers. Just the one where I lived. 'White or wholemeal?' He made good pies as well, almost as good as the tuck shop, almost. The tuck shop ones were really good but getting your teeth into a pie required pocket money and that was rationed, severely. An after school job helped, but that was hard, clashed with sports practise and the like, left little time to be with your mates, kept you out of trouble though.

That morning bread run had its moments; wintertime. I lived down south, wintertime was cold, frost and ice. There were no cars, everyone had a bike. Balaclavas, gloves, chilblains, cold sores, it could be very cold some mornings.

'The bread, the sandwiches.'

'Ok Mum, I'm on my way, I'll be back in time.' God is it ever cold this morning.

'And don't pick a hole in it or you'll get a clip in the ear.'

'No Mum.'

There's ice on the road the bike can go for a real skate on that stuff, better ride on the grass verge.

That morning bread run, a regular routine. There was the morning when I got my hand caught in the heavy glass door that kept the baker's shop so nice and warm, deep cut on the thumb, blood everywhere. The baker was very good, big plaster, phoned mum.

'It's ok Mum, I can pedal home, don't worry.'

Suddenly the pain vanished, he gave me a hot meat pie, life was complete. I wonder if I can pull that stunt again?

That big glass door got me on another occasion. Summertime, hot day, bare feet; running around barefoot was quite normal when I was a kid. The bread run, in a hurry, not paying attention. It was big and heavy that glass door, had an automatic closing device as well. My toe was in the way, it just fitted under the door, well not quite, the nail was torn right off, blood everywhere again. Not endearing myself to the baker. This time he was very concerned, bandages, phone mum again.

It hurt like the devil, and the blood! Yes Mr Baker, I can pedal home, really I can, it will be ok, don't think I can handle a pie though. I was feeling a bit crook, he'd not offered one anyway. Made it home with the bread intact, no holes, but the toe was really hurting. School's going to be difficult today, don't have to wear shoes though. That was yesteryear; fortunately for the baker OSH did not exist!

Bikes; everyone had a bike, that's how we got around, that's how we got the bread. Cars were rare, could not buy a car, had to go on a waiting list, wait for years. It was a bike, good for you, kept you fit and healthy. At school there was a huge bike rack but if you were late all the spaces were gone and your bike would have to spend the day up against the fence.

There was no real safety issue riding a bike. There were very few cars to cause problems. When school finished a great tsunami of cyclists flooded out from the school grounds. No one ever got picked up from school in a car.

I enjoyed pedalling my bike, unless the weather intervened, which it did from time to time. A howling nor'wester, heavy rain, and you had to pedal into it. We did have the right clothing however, raincoats and hats, do you know what a raincoat is? It's a waterproof garment you wear over your clothes when you go to school on a wet day. I don't think they make them anymore! The world is a changing place I know, but I do have a problem with kids and raincoats. How can they sit in a classroom all day in wet clothes?

Breakfast rolls, come across them? They come in little packets, small and delicious, just pop in the oven and bingo, a real little taste thrill, eat immediately. The latest find, and this is a really good one, home baked bread. 'Hang on we've been through the bread making era.' 'I know, but this is different.' A boating mate told me about this frozen dough he'd found, came in the form of a roll about fifteen centimetres long, ideal for the freezer, doesn't take up much space. The idea is to make the bread when it's required, 'darned good bread too, here, try a couple.' We did, he was right, excellent bread.

'So where did you get it?'

'You can't buy it normally, it's the dough some supermarkets use to make their bread.'

'But they have their own bakers who do it all, don't they?' 'Not always, sometimes they buy it in.'

'So what's the secret?'

'Ok, go along to that supermarket down by the river. At the bakery ask for Jean, she's the contact, you'll probably have to buy a complete box of the stuff.'

Off I went.

'Is Jean available?'

'Yep, I'll get her.'

Jean turns out to be a character, I think she was Rarotongan. I make my inquiry about these small frozen rolls of dough that come in boxes of, I think, forty eight pieces.

'Yes, I think I've seen them,' she says, not giving much away.

'Well I would like to buy some, is that possible?'

'We don't normally sell them, I'll have to ask the boss. Yep, the boss say's that's ok, but you'll have to buy a whole box.'

'I didn't see any boss?' I comment.

'I'm the boss today, I'm the boss everyday,' she chuckles away, big grin.

'What do you want it for?' she asks.

'It's for a boat, with this stuff you can have fresh bread every day, great idea.'

'That sounds good, a complete box?'

'Done deal, how will I pay?'

'I'll write the price on the box. You just tell the check out girl that Jean said that's what it is.'

This frozen dough is great, take it out, leave it sitting at room temperature for a bit. It thaws and rises, rises a lot, then into the oven for a short bake. Delicious hot fresh bread and I thought all bakers were clever.

The local baker, everyone has a favourite, ours is a franchise one. It's good, loyalty cards, promotions, coupon deals, half price after five, 'but there's nothing left by five.' It's a real friendly place, does a roaring trade. But then Auckland is a friendly place, well it is out in the suburbs where the real people live. Our baker is next to the Lotto shop. Quite often, when I pick up a loaf I have a newly purchased *winning* lotto ticket in my hand. Every ticket's a winning one isn't it? Until Saturday night that is. Buy it on a Monday, enjoy a whole week of expectation.

'We're doing two for eight dollars right now.'

'I only want one, but thanks for the offer.'

'You could freeze it!'

'Yes I could, but I only want the one; it's the add on isn't it?' She smiles and nods her head.

'That another winning ticket I see in your hand?'

'Yep, come Sunday I just might buy all your bread, and your shop, if only!'

'Dear would you drive up to the bread shop and get a white high fibre, toast sliced, please.' No bike these days, too life threatening.

'Yes dear.'

'Oh, and see if they've got any of that Turkish bread, the ones that come in a packet of six, would you?'

'Yes dear.'

'White or wholemeal sir?'

They say your long term memory is the last thing to fail!

The Urban Tank

It's big, black, and aggressive. Covered with chrome, huge pretentious bull bars and it's completely filling my rear view mirror. I can imagine the salivating driver thinking about running me off the road. What is it with these people who have to have an urban tank to intimidate the road users in Auckland, and the bull bars?

The SUV, the 4x4, the off roader, whatever you like to call these monsters that some males foist upon their families. Why must they have one? Poor wifey, she has to use it to do the shopping. The ultimate male ego trip. What's missing in their lives, are they so frustrated with their lot that they have to run around intimidating everyone else on the road? They're so big, total vision block when one pulls alongside and they always seem to tailgate you, is it the elevated driving position or just the personality of the driver? We seem to be cursed with an abundance of the things, the ideal vehicle for our congested roads!

The supermarket car park. Poor wifey has been stuck with this thing to do the shopping, how do I park it? It's just too big, everyone is glaring at me. How do I climb down out of it and still retain a little of my dignity? I loved our little Bimmer, then *he* decides we're going to get a SUV, not any old SUV, a seriously big one. The damned thing only just fits in the garage, I've already scraped the brickwork. This insistence on a SUV coincided with his deciding to join the gym, mid forties, it's true, midlife crisis. It'll be facial hair next, heaven forbid. Some good may come out of it though, that bulge above his belt, won't go with the leotards. Perhaps he should have done a stretch in the army, they have real tanks. Could have worked out his frustration there and I could still go shopping in the Bimmer. Is this the man I married? The kids are of two minds. Peter thinks it's pretty neat, but Rebecca is disgusted. 'Dad and his toy, we don't have a real car anymore,' as for being picked up from school when it's pelting down, well it doesn't happen, the thing's too big for Mum to handle in the usual mayhem outside our school on a wet afternoon.

Why are there so many SUVs on our roads? They would have to be the most impractical vehicle for urban driving. Auckland males seem to have a love affair with the SUV, the bigger the better, some of them are ridiculously big. Some even have great black air sucking gadgets on the outside so they can keep going when submerged and an array of floodlights across the top of the cab, real handy in Auckland's traffic. They guzzle fuel, tyres cost an arm and a leg, they're a dog to drive and servicing costs are way way up, so what have they got going for them? Very little except they seem to have a huge appeal to the male ego, an insight into the JAFFA mind set.

The other day I saw a Hummer with canvas doors, the ultimate urban tank. I hasten to add not all Auckland males go along with this, I can't stand the things, my ego does not demand a 4x4. There are more enjoyable ways to get your kicks, a monster road vehicle is not one of them.

Well you have my opinion. I pity the poor spouses who are stuck with one of these things, straight out lack of consideration I reckon. I wonder what domestics precede the purchase? We live in a changing world, it sure does change, and quickly, so perhaps girls, there's hope. Something else may come along that's got greater appeal than a 4x4, perhaps then you'll be able to make a case for the Bimmer.

The Ticket

They arrived in the mailbox on a cold wet windy morning, two letters from the New Zealand Police, *the Police;* that grabbed the attention, concentrated the mind, quickened the pulse. A sudden uneasy feeling, *am I in trouble?* Can't be, I'm a law abiding citizen, I don't get into trouble, I'm a good guy. Suddenly I feel very uncomfortable, stressed, what can the police possibly want with me?

It's a speeding ticket, actually two speeding tickets, two separate speeding fines, two criminal offences. I don't speed, I conform, I have been socially engineered, there must be some mistake. No mistake, two thirty dollar fines for exceeding the fifty kilometre speed limit, both offences committed at the same spot, the same speed camera, two crimes against society separated by just sixty minutes, this cannot be right. Read the fine print, when and where did these heinous crimes take place. It was at the bottom of a hill, a fairly steep hill. If you don't brake, brake quite heavily, you will be going too fast. I was not going too fast, I do brake on that hill. Fifty-six kilometres per hour and fifty-seven sir, in a fifty kilometre speed zone, you were *speeding*. It was a trap, a revenue gathering exercise, it had to be, how very unfair.

What's speeding anyway, it's going too fast, is fifty-six fast? Suppose it depends whose side you're on. Come on now, going downhill, a car just naturally accelerates, sure you brake but fifty-six, come on, that's what everyone does down that hill. Whatever happened to common sense, reasonableness, the real world. Ah, this is the real world sir, you were speeding, $30 please; *twice!*

It was a heavily disguised van with tinted windows, a big camera that you could not see through the tint, I know because I spotted it again a week later, same place, same revenue gathering exercise. entrapment, not fair.

Please pay on or before the 29th at the bank, penalties apply for late payment. I present myself to the cashier, this agent of the devil, the collector of this innovative additional tax imposed on the motorist by a rapacious administration.

'Don't you feel guilty doing this' I say with a smile, after all she's not the villain here, just the villain's servant.

'No, I'm immune, I need to be, there's been a stream of people in here this morning just like you.'

'Really, the criminalization of the innocent.'

'Yep that's exactly what it is.'

We examine my two tickets and note that the numbering is separated by 59 digits, 1042 and 1101. Does this mean that in just sixty minutes the camera clicked 60 times, once a minute, 60 times $30, $1,800 in an hour. A forty hour week would return $72,000, yep, that's revenue gathering from *speeding* motorists all of whom were doing just a bit over fifty. That's pretty serious stuff, the punch line; just a couple of hundred metres up the road from this speed trap, this state approved revenue gatherer, it's not a criminal offence, there's a sixty kilometre speed sign.

I'm in the wrong business, I should contract myself to the state as a speed entrapment person, sort out all the steep roads around town, take a percentage, buy into the disc brake business, there's serious money here. A punitive tax imposed on the law abiding.

We've all experienced it, what, not you? Rubbish, everyone gets clobbered sometime. It's just not possible to avoid, part of our life style, something to talk about at the pub, the dinner party, wherever. 'And how much did you get stung for, what, that much, you must be a really bad person.' We try, well I do, I've been socially engineered remember, but it still happens, out of nowhere a speeding ticket. The slightest moment of inattention, a drifting of the mind, and in the latest engineering marvel, all the extras, super quiet, cost an arm and a leg. It just accelerates all by itself, turns you into a criminal, a person with a police record, threatens your licence, demerit points, better watch it or you'll be on your bike, banned from the public highways, a menace in a motor car, a bad person.

What's happened to our society, never used to be like this in the olden days. Speeding tickets, they were something you only heard about and it was usually for some horrendous speeding offence involving an accident wasn't it? in the olden days. The olden days when everything was perfect, every day was sunny, nothing went wrong, life was good. The local Policeman was your friend, Mum and Dad knew him. He had a beaut daughter, Sarah, I had a crush on her, wonder what happened to Sarah? But that was in small town New Zealand, south of the Bombay's where the real people live. Blenheim, across Cook Strait. Now I'm grown up and live in Auckland where people are not so friendly, not very white either. Different to Blenheim, driving is not enjoyable, one continuous traffic jam and everyone speeds. Traffic cops are anonymous creatures, not real members of the community, not your friends. Out to get you seems to be their thing and they do get you. They're sneaky. Speed traps at the bottom of hills, how sneaky is that? Not like the olden days at all. Perhaps I should move out of the big city, go south of the Bombay's, go all the way back to Blenheim where people are friendly and the sun always shines, well it used to didn't it? I did go south, I visited the relly's the other day in Blenheim, drove down, needed a car when I got there so I thought I would take mine and enjoy a drive through heartland New Zealand where the nice people live. Would you believe two speeding tickets, two $30 ones, the nasty revenue gatherers have enlarged their hunting grounds, spread their tentacles south of the Bombay's, nowhere is safe from these rapacious tax gatherers. It got worse, childhood memories were shattered, Blenheim, it bucketed down and I got pinged again, 57k sir in a 50k zone, a menace to society.

The world is changing and I'm beginning to think I must be an old fart!

Dog

The tail's a blur, overjoyed to see me, talking flat out. The routine never varies, big lick, I love the little creature.

He just goes away, leaves me locked in the kitchen. Then he's back and I'm so happy. I tell him, but he doesn't understand. I lick his leg. I like licking his leg, even better if there's a broken bit. He pats my head, wish he wouldn't do that, I think he's going to hit me but he would never do that, prefer a pat on the back.

She's a Bichon Frisé, a little white fluff ball, a rug rat. We got her at six months, put a lot of time in early on, now she's four. Thinks she's human, mimics our every move, a creature of habit. Close observer of our every move. Got to be in the same room, follows us around the house, loves company, eats when we eat, always trying for the same plate, never gives up.

'Yours is in your bowl.'

'I know, but it tastes better off your plate.'

I've lived here with my mum and dad forever. They talk to me and mum is always fussing around brushing my wool, even washes me. I'm always happy, well nearly always. When I'm not happy the only way I can let them know is to do something that gets their attention. I think it must be wrong to do this because they always seem to be a bit annoyed when I piddle inside.

What is it about a dog? That much hackneyed saying, man's best friend, it's true. I think they need our friendship more than we need theirs, a totally devoted friendship, something you could never betray. This little fellow adores us, that's a big responsibility. A dog, will never argue, you're always right, well almost always, it loves you no matter what, it's your best mate, a little oasis of unquestioning love in our stress filled world.

Do you have a dog? no? You're missing one of life's most rewarding experiences. Your love is returned tenfold, it's quite incredible, man's best friend indeed.

People tell you dogs smell, they're messy, could be right, but not Bichons, they don't smell and they don't make a mess, well that's not quite true either. They don't make the usual dog hair mess, but they can definitely transgress in the toilet department, in fact at times it's almost deliberate.

'You've not been nice to me, I'll show you!'

Talk to your dog, they understand. They try to do the right thing, but they're like us, human, behavioural aberrations do occur.

'You little sod, what's this piddle on the carpet?'

'But it's raining.'

'No excuse, you know the rules, outside, now.' The tail's stopped wagging.

Smell, the doggy kind, there isn't any with a Bichon, they've got a woolly coat, woolly creatures don't smell. Being such delightful little darlings they assume they have rights. They don't take no for an answer, *'I sleep on the bed, end of story.'* Well that's Bichons, other dogs are different, different all right, how about a fishing dog.

It happened at Muri Beach in Rarotonga, that jewel of the South Seas so popular with Kiwis. A long walk on the white sand in the warmth of the morning sun, and in July. Paddling along in the ripples where the ocean, the big blue Pacific Ocean, laps the sand, there are these small almost translucent fish right up in the ripples, practically invisible, a lot of them when you look closely. A couple of Blue Herons poised gracefully, purposefully, breakfast time. As we move along the beach the local dogs come out for a look when we enter their patch. All shapes and sizes, small yappies to big mean looking types, all very friendly. Plenty of wet nose rubs, the odd lick and a general desire to just walk along with us. We are well along the beach when we see it. Poised motionless in the shallows, three legs in the water, the fourth raised, the hunting posture. Not the slightest movement, like one of those street buskers who paint themselves silver and stand on the pavement motionless. It's quite a big dog, and it's frozen, staring into the water, just like a Heron. It's fishing, those little translucent fish the Herons are hunting. Dog is in on the act. Evolution has equipped the Herons rather well for fishing, not sure about dog. We walk on, dog does not move. It's exhilarating just walking along the beach, then the sky darkens, a storm cloud moves in, turn around, go back before the heavens open up. Fishing dog is still there, has he moved? Any fish? There's a young lad on the beach, we ask about 'fishing dog.'

'Oh the dog; it's always doing that, caught a fish once.'
I gathered fishing dog did not enjoy too much success, but ten out of ten for dedication. We went for a walk the following day, fishing dog was not there.

Bones, synthetic or real, dog likes them all, we tend towards the synthetic, cleaner. It's a serious consideration because they turn up in the most unlikely places. Dog buries them wherever she thinks they will remain undiscovered, in the bed, under the bed, behind cushions, under pillows.

They'll never find this one, I'll push it down the back of the settee, should be safe there, they'll never look. How will I get it out? Perhaps I pushed it down a bit far, better pull it out now before I forget where I hid it. Can't get it out, If I dig a bit I might get it. That big brown one I buried some time ago, can't find it now. Those ones that don't taste like a real bone, no smell, how's a dog supposed to find them, my memory's a bit poor at times, I can usually remember where I put them. I'm digging, can't get it, whoops here comes Mum.

'What are you doing on the sofa?'

'Digging up my bone and I can't quite get it.'

'I see, there's a bone down there.'

'Yes Mum.'

'Here, let me get it for you.'

Mum's so kind she digs down, success, the bone sees the light of day. About the big brown one, can you find that for me? How can I ask? I talk to Mum but she doesn't understand. That's not fair, I understand what she says, I talk a lot, Dad says I'm a real chatterbox, whatever that means.

Burying bones is a full time occupation for dog, she's always at it and it's always inside. Going to bed at night can be interesting, how did she get this one down under the bedding, ouch, there's a lump under the pillow as well and going to the toilet in the dark can be tough on the feet sometimes, ever trodden heavily on a bone?

They're going out, I can tell, they're washing and dressing. They do a lot of washing, Mum even washes me sometimes, what's wrong with a good licking. I offer to lick them, frequently. Looks like the dog bed in the kitchen again. It's a good bed, I like it, spend a lot of time sleeping there during the day, never at night though, there's a much better bed, really big, in the room at the end of the hall where Mum and Dad sleep, that's for me at night. If tonight follows the usual pattern it will be a few hours in the kitchen. Sometimes they come home very late when I'm sound asleep, I get a bit of a fright when suddenly they're towering over me, but it's always good to have them home again. They close the kitchen doors when they go out, reckon I might piddle on the carpet if I'm left with the run of the house. I'd never do that, only if they have been nasty to me, then I might, I'll show them. There's a dog door that lets me out into the backyard, that's great, my own private toilet and play area. I can go out there and give the neighbours a good woofing when Mum and Dad are out, they'll never know.

Locked up, dog in the kitchen, doors closed, back in a couple of hours. It's Wednesday, regular dinner group, always a good feed on Wednesday, been doing it for years.

'Won't be long dog, see you in a wee while.'

They're home, I'm happy, don't like being left alone, need company. I like Mum and Dad to be home, I follow them around, I like to be in the same room.

'Right, bedtime, come on dog, outside, toilet.'

This is a regular routine. They want me to go outside and pee before I leap into their big bed. I pee on the damp grass out the front, rather like the feel of the damp grass on my bottom. If I jump off the bed during the night and take off down the hall Mum gets out of bed and follows me. She reckons I'm lazy and won't bother to go outside, easier to pee in the hall, this makes her angry. But I always go out through the dog door, well nearly always. When it's raining the hall's an easier option. I don't think Mum trusts me.

'Thunk,' my lead drops to the floor in front of me, a good sign, it means Dad's going to take me for a walk, hopefully a long walk. I get excited and start jumping all over him, he seems to like it. A walk, I'll get to go through that gate down the front, the one that stops me from running away. I run away, don't know why, I just do, can't help myself. The last time I got through that gate Dad chased me, great game, we went all the way into the village with Dad in hot pursuit. He was yelling something about grab that dog and someone did, picked me up right off the ground. Dad caught up, puffing, not very pleased.

'Thank you so much, you've saved my skin.'

'Not a problem, I've got one of these too, I know the problem.'

Dad puts the choker lead around my neck, don't like it, it hurts. When I try to drag Dad along he jerks it and says 'heel.' Off we go, down to the bottom of the road, will he turn around and go back, the short walk, no he's turning right, joy oh joy, it's the long walk, right around the block. I love this one, so much to see, gets a bit boring at home all the time. There's a big garden at home, lots of grubby places where I can play, but it's not the same as the long walk. Woof, woof, that's the big black dog, always barks when I go past. Just as well he's fenced in otherwise I would tear his throat out if he had a go at me. I ignore big black. I used to give him a good woofing but Dad didn't like it and I always try to please Dad. There's that cat, it's always there tormenting me, scruffy little thing. I make a lunge, ouch, the chocker really hurts as Dad gives it a sharp tug. Why do you do that Dad, I only want to take a chunk out of that cat, it's natural, instinctive. Onto the main road, I can feel Dad's grip tighten on the leash, all that traffic. Dad says I have no road sense, whatever that means. On we go, be turning for home shortly. Some school children approach from the opposite direction. I like new people, I like all people. Dad says I would be useless as a guard dog. That's not very nice Dad. I can make a lot of noise, usually do whenever someone I don't know comes up the drive. You want to see those Bible Bangers turn and flee, great sport. School children, they're always nice to me, well the girls are, the boys can be a bit surly. These are girls, I'm going to be made a fuss of.

'Can we pat the dog please.'

'Surely.'

They do make a fuss, I knew they would, I jump all over them, lots of licks, they say things like 'Ug, it tickles.' I like new people.

Home, bit tired, that was a long walk. I think Dad likes doing it as well, bit of exercise I heard him say. Race inside and drain my water bowl. When it's empty I shove it around the kitchen floor making as much noise as possible. That gets their attention, the bowl gets filled. I drink a lot of water, something to pee with.

'Pets,' it's the name of a holiday place. I go there quite a bit, it's great. Sometimes my little sister is there as well. She lives around the corner. Her Mum and Dad are friendly with my Mum and Dad, they

all go away together sometimes. When this happens it's 'Pets' for us and it's great. Lots of other dogs, not Bichons, but we all have a great time, not like those dog club gatherings Mum takes me to, they're all Bichons and they annoy me, no reason, they just do. The odd one is nice, but most are not, so I have a go at them. Mum seems to be annoyed when I do this but if I don't like another dog I let it know.

We have a boat, a big launch, dog loves it, take her along every time. Gets seasick though and it's always that first hour out from the marina, we're ready for it, towels in place. After the one episode, that's it, no further problem, she just enjoys herself. Swimming, loves it, but we restrict it to beaches, would not want her hopping off the duckboard. A swim in the shallows on some remote beach, a run in the sand, a real sandy mess, and a hosing down on the duckboard, just loves the whole experience. Seabirds, they can be pretty cheeky, hop onto the duckboard sometimes, that always gets a vigorous response, dog in water can result. Good with the fishing, just sits and watches, no getting hooked, does get excited when something's thrashing about in the fish bin though and when a Kahawai is landed be careful, they can spray a lot of blood about, that gets dog's attention.

Yipee we're off down to the marina, I can tell, I know these things. It's the boat, I love the boat. A pee on the marina walkway and we're off, very noisy. Oops, don't feel too good, I think I'm going to throw up. Mum's all ready with a big towel, she's very perceptive. I do throw up, a big throw, all that breakfast, don't know why I do it, must be the excitement, after all, with any luck I could be on this boat with Mum and Dad for several days. I wonder how long it will be this time, they never tell me. Can sometimes get an idea by the amount of food they take along, but they seem to take heaps every time. There will be fishing and swimming, swimming! I love swimming, get to do my dog paddle in the shallows, and I can get into a real sandy mess running around on a beach, it's great fun. There's the hosing down, I like that bit. Not allowed inside though until I'm all clean and tidy, bit unfair, I would love to spread a bit of sand around the cabin, get some into the bed, that would be fun. I see we're getting a bit close to my sister's Mum and Dad's boat, I think it's going to be another one of those noisy evenings. That's the anchor, I know that noise. It is a noisy evening. They've tied the backs of the two boats together and they're having a sundowner, whatever that is, they usually have something called cocktail hour. Can't tell the difference, both involve drinking something called wine and beer, hope they feed me before they get beyond it, because sometimes they do.

They say burglars avoid yappy dogs. We're safe, our dog is very yappy. If a burglar turned up then this little puff ball would make a lot of noise, but then, after a bit, she would just lick him to death, she just likes people. When talking with the neighbours I try and mention that we are aware the dog can be noisy at times, but it does keep the burglars away.

I've told you how much I like licking Dad, always sniffing out the broken bits, they taste good. Well the other day Dad presented me with a real feast, like winning Doggy Lotto, it doesn't get any better. He was mucking around in the garden heaving big bags of stuff about with a trolley affair, next minute he's sitting on the ground and there's blood everywhere, lots of blood. Does not look right, better check it out. Dad is looking a bit sad and holding his leg, blood is pouring out, I like blood, I'll just give this offering a try, very tasty. Dad mutters something about bloody vampire dog, what about giving me a hand, what can I do, I'm a dog. We were home alone, Dad's on his own with this one. He fumbled around with a towel and some tape stuff, I think he called it duct tape, left a trail of blood everywhere. Not a problem, I cleaned up after him, it was good. I've never had such a good feed of rich red blood before. Dad did not look so good though, he disappeared in the car shortly afterwards. I continued cleaning up, there was quite a bit to do. When I next saw him, some hours later, he had two extra legs, metal things he called crutches, he looked funny moving around. He was not happy, pretty miserable, so I jumped on him and gave him a big lick, this left a big red stain on his clothes. I don't think he was very happy about that either. He said my face was covered with blood and shortly after that he's got this flannel and he's washing my face. This seemed to exhaust him, not like Dad, he collapsed on the settee in the front room. I was now getting a bit concerned, the vibes were not good, better be extra nice. I'll sit on him and give him another lick. I've just had a thought, this could put an end to the walks around the block, wonder how long before Dad gets over this?

Crutches for a few days, keep the foot elevated, nasty wound, lot of stitches. Plenty of reading time coming up, have to keep off the leg for a while.

One week on, all ok, well on the way to recovery, dog has been great company. There will be a reward, an extra long walk, she just loves going for a walk. Another couple of days, perhaps a bit longer and I'll be right. Bit annoyed with myself, an accident, it's cost me a few days. Been bucketing down for most of the time so you could say the timing was good; one way of looking at it.

Dad's not taken me walking yet, still spending a lot of time lying on the settee in the front room reading, I think his leg is still troubling him, better do my own exercise routine, some fast running around the place. I'm off, flat out down the hall, back, out the door, leap down the two steps in front of the veranda, off around the lawn, just as fast as I can go. Dad says I'm doing the Bichon run, he says all Bichons do this, it's a behavioural thing, whatever that means. I do this circuit several times then suddenly I'm worn out, have to stop and lie down. I enjoy the Bichon run but I like a walk with Dad more, please hurry up and get better.

The bird feeder. There's this box affair hanging in a tree outside above the lawn, Mum puts bread in. I like bread, she says it's for the birds. They fly down and peck away at it, sometimes the bread falls down onto the lawn. When this happens I race out, grab it, and carry it off into the garden where Mum can't see me and eat it. Sometimes, if there's a really big piece, I will sneak inside with it. Have to avoid Mum though because she will tick me off and take it off me. I like to bury the big pieces in a good place, under one of the pillows on the big bed is a good spot. When we all go to bed at night Mum and Dad seem to be amused by the things they find under the bedclothes and quite often it's not until the early hours before there's a grumble as they discover a lump under a pillow, another bone, one they missed earlier.

Today Mum is taking me to Tauranga. This is unbelievably exciting, we have done it before, my sister is coming too. We are going to a dog show where we will meet all these other dogs that live in Tauranga. We stay in something called a motel where dogs are welcome. I would have thought dogs would be welcome anywhere but apparently this is not the case. Some motels don't allow dogs, that's pretty mean. My sister's Mum is coming as well, she always comes to Tauranga when we go there. It's a long trip in a car, I like the car, it takes me to different places, I like that. Dad does not come to these dog shows, he says it's not his thing anyway; he still has a crook leg so he would not be much use, he couldn't take me for walks in Tauranga.

Every so often Mum takes me along to this place where a nice lady cuts a lot of my wool off with some electric clipper things. Mum calls it grooming. I have wool, not smelly dog hair. Not sure I like this grooming but I do like the end result. People say I look very smart after grooming, whatever that means. What I do notice is the cold after a grooming, ok when it's warm though. There's one thing I find very strange about this grooming, there's always discussion about the size of my head, that's weird, my head does not change size.

There's one thing I like a lot, it's when this small person visits and makes a fuss over me. I like being fussed over. They call this small person Rosie or granddaughter, I think her name is really Rosie, she's small, well she was small, not much bigger than me but every time I see her she's bigger. Rosie picks me up and carries me around, I like that. Mum is always giving her food called chippies. Rosie drops these chippies on the kitchen floor quite often and I gobble them up real quick before anyone notices, they're good these chippies.

The coffee table in the lounge, a place where we sit and enjoy a coffee, perhaps a piece of cake, a place where we put nibbles when we have people around which is quite often, in fact the coffee table is a place where there is frequently food.

They've left the room, moved to the kitchen, there's food on the coffee table, even better, some empty coffee cups. They'll not be completely empty, there's always lovely fluffy milk, sugar sometimes, in the bottom of these cups. I'll just hop up on the table and scoff the lot. Need to be quick though, they'll be back, if I'm caught there will be hell to play. Crash, bugger, I've knocked a coffee cup over.

'What do you think you're doing, off there you little blighter.'
It's Dad, caught red handed, Dad's not happy, he's called me a little blighter as well, don't know what that means but I don't think it's a good sign, better just vanish. Oops, don't feel good, I'm out on the deck hiding, oops, I think I'm going to be sick, I am sick, big mess, it's that cheese stuff, I think that's what it's called, there was a big

round piece on a plate, I woofed it down, had to be quick. That's better, got rid of it all, bit of a mess though, I'll be in trouble if Mum finds this. Smells pretty good that cheese stuff perhaps I could eat it again, can't just leave this mess for Mum to find. Yes it does taste good and I don't have to woof it down, can take my time. All gone, two meals for one, deck all clean, they will never know.

Dog, I love the little creature, naughtiness and all, I'm sure my time on this earth will be extended by having Dog in my life. There are times though when I think she's a bit lonely, needs some dog company perhaps, now there's a thought.

My Skin Don't Fit

It's true, it doesn't fit any more, there's too much of it, all loose and wrinkly and it doesn't look nice, what's happened? You've aged, that's what's happened and there's precious little you can do about it.

Realisation hit hard one day at the beach when a good friend commented.

'What's happened to your skin?'

'What do you mean?'

He had a point, when I had a serious look it was not good, there was too much skin, loose, surplus, yuk!

I'm well beyond my three score years and ten, old, and not acknowledging it, in denial, all in the mind I keep telling myself. You're only as old as you think you are. Think old and you'll be old. Look around, how often do you see just that.

It crept up on me, subtle changes, lost a bit of weight, good thing, but same skin, too much of it, surplus, why does it just not shrink to fit, but it doesn't, it just stays the same, and it's all wrinkly. Does it worry me? Not really. As I've grown older I have noticed subtle changes in my attitude to life, I don't care about some things any more. Nothing you can do about it, accept the fact that you are no longer a Charles Atlas, were you ever? Who's Charles Atlas? I guess I am old. The eyesight, not the greatest either, nature's way of protecting you from seeing yourself perhaps, add in poor hearing as well, can't hear the comments. Am I becoming paranoid? No not me, I'm immune to all that, it's just that as the years pass certain physical things become apparent that annoy me.

My skin don't fit!

Recently we went on a cruise, the ship's swimming pool featured large. What to do, up there with the beautiful people. I'm aware of my skin, how can I mingle with the beautiful people? I'd given away the budgie smugglers years ago, older men in Jockey's, disgusting. Not me, it's been board pants for years, commando sometimes.

My skin? what the heck, I don't care, just go ahead, enjoy the moment, appearances are only skin deep. Well yes, but all those beautiful people?

Saved, there's a fellow just like me. Pretty obvious he's long got over any complex about wrinkly skin. When I observed further there were more, in fact there were quite a lot of 'wrinklies.' They are not all beautiful people on this boat, there are lots of people with great character, older people, just like me.

Is it vanity, do we have to have perfectly fitting skin, after all it's just there to keep our insides in and that brings up another matter, this wrinkly skin does a poor job of keeping my insides in. I'm constantly springing leaks, just a touch and it tears, blood, I'm leaking again. More Johnson plasters, I buy them in boxes of fifty these days. I've taken to wearing gloves as well, thin vinyl ones, whenever I go inside the engine bay on the boat, or under the car bonnet. Failure to wear gloves results in bloody hands and lots of plasters. It's a fact of life, you don't get thick skinned as you get older, definitely not, the stuff gets very thin and fragile, believe me.

What can be done? Steroids will bulk you up, fill your skin, return you to the Charles Atlas of your youth. Forget it, that's heart failure stuff. Eat more perhaps, well I do eat, plenty at times, nothing happens, in fact if I don't eat, the weight, what there is of it, drops off even more, can't win!

My skin don't fit.

Pump iron, that'll do it, someone told me, pump iron, bulk up, fill that skin. There are a couple of dumb bells in a cupboard in the study, you know, those things that are great for the arms, and shoulders, used them a lot once. They seem to be a bit heavier these days, what can it be, dust perhaps.

The gym, that's the story, get down to the gym, get into it, pump iron, hang on, won't there be a bit of a generation gap? Used to go to the gym years ago, I was a bit on the old side then. It's a youngies place, leotards and lycra, is that me? Is there an age limit? Perhaps I should have kept it up, not stopped when I did, should have kept my skin filled.

And something else, my trousers have become baggy. Same trousers that I've had for a while, they used to look smart on me but now they're baggy, definitely not smart, why is this? My friends tell me I've got no bum, nothing to fill them out, too much material at the back and no bum.

My skin don't fit, and neither do my trousers.

Some years ago a close friend died from a wasting disease, it was awful, he just wasted away to skin and bone over a period of a few months and died. No cure, random chance, real unlucky, could that be me? No never. If I make an effort and really pig out, like on a cruise ship, I actually put on weight, but the moment I back off the eating it all falls off again, and my bum never quite fills my trousers.

Spinach, I like spinach, eat it quite often, now I find out it's an appetite killer, there's something in spinach that kills the appetite. That figures, I don't have much of an appetite, no big craving to eat, in fact I can go all day without eating a thing, it does not bother me at all. 'Popeye' ate spinach, he was skinny. Who's Popeye? He's right up there with Charles Atlas, you're too young to know.

Looks like I'm stuck with it, no quick fix, my skin's too big and it won't shrink. I'm not worrying about it though, my burden to carry. You younger folk, something to look forward too, one day your skin won't fit either and that raises another thing, tattoos.

56 My Skin Don't Fit

You're young, perfectly formed body, skin fits, get a tattoo, in thing, trendy, have to be a trendy.

Fifty years on, bugger, how do I get rid of this distorted mess.

A parting thought, well an observation really, there are no fat old people, ever noticed?

That's A Faucet Sir

'Hello sir, can I help you?'
'Yes, I'm looking for a tap.'
'Excuse me?'
'A tap.'
'I don't think we have taps sir.'
'Yes you do, there's one over there.'
'Sir, that's a faucet.'

They're different, Americans, they're different. When it comes to plumbing, very different. I was in a huge plumbing warehouse in downtown Honolulu looking for a tap, a flash hot and cold aerated job, can't get anything like it in New Zealand. It's the 1960s, I'm building a house, my very first house, you know the one where everything is going to be perfect. In the 60s there was precious little that was 'flash' available in New Zealand. Trips abroad were invariably spent buying things you could not get in New Zealand, a country of 'have not,' or more correctly 'can't get.' Import licensing, horrendous duty imposts and just plain, *'no you can't have it,'* and here I was confronted with a mind numbingly huge display of bathroom taps; 'it's a faucet sir.' A faucet for every conceivable purpose, hot, cold, mixing, aerated, temperature controlling, flow adjustable, brass, plated, stainless, gold plated, high lift, low lift, wall mounted, flush mounted, you name it, it's available. Overwhelming to a naïve young lad from the South Seas, from the land of 'have not.'

'Thank you, I'll have a look around.'

It's all a bit much, spoilt for choice. What do I want, I'm confused by what's on offer, having trouble comprehending. It didn't stop with taps, sorry faucets, there were toilets, bidets, hand basins, showers, overhead heaters, extractor fans, heated towel rails, baths, perhaps I'll confine myself to taps, sorry faucets.

Faucet, my mind wanders, dizzy blonde, drop dead gorgeous, Farrah!

Toilet or bathroom, I'm confused again, Americans seem to be confused as well. It seems to depend on where the actual thing you sit on, the toilet, is located, if it's the bathroom, that's the room where the bath is, then that room is called a toilet, if not, then it's a bathroom, I think.

'Excuse me where's the toilet?' and you're directed to a bathroom, there's no toilet there, I'm confused!

The salad and the main course, come across this one, very different. No meat until you've eaten your salad. Reminds me of my childhood, no pudding until-----. Let me tell you about an amusing incident.

We were in this restaurant in middle America, a steak house, a good one. It was the first time outside New Zealand for one of our group and he was struggling. There's this selection of steaks on offer. I was not familiar with some of the dishes on the menu myself and our 'new boy' was definitely out of his comfort zone. Orders were placed and we settled down with a beer or two while we waited for the meal, nothing happened!

'Excuse me,' it's the waiter.

'Would you like to go along to the salad bar now please.'

'Ah yes, alright.'

'When I see you have your salads I will start your meal.'

An excellent salad bar, I piled my plate high, plenty of avocado, I love avocado, blue cheese dressing, don't see that back home. Back to our table with all this salad. I start in on it, perhaps if I knock all this off I can go back for some more avocado and blue cheese dressing. Our 'new chum' is holding back, not eating his salad.

After a while our waiter advises that our meals are almost ready.

'Are you finished with the salad?' the waiter asks, his comments directed to our 'newbie.'

'No, I'm waiting for my steak.'

'Sir, I will bring your steak when you have finished your salad.'

'What? I want my steak with my salad.'

'Oh, that's not normal here, however, if that's what you want I will bring the meals now.'

There's a noticeable note of disdain in the waiter's voice.

'Thank you.'

Our new chum's response is a bit curt.

The meals arrive and they look quite superb, big steaks done to perfection, this will be good.

The waiter puts on a bit of a show when presenting the meal to our new chum, I think he had twigged he had a bit of a 'hayseed' here, it got even better when our mate eyed his steak. It was big, done to perfection, and it had an orange 'thing' on top. There was a short silence, all eyes on our new chum who, after a bit, took his fork and cautiously prodded the orange 'thing.'

'Christ, it's a peach!'

Indeed it was, a steak with a peach on top, a common dish in the American Midwest, that's what our mate had unwittingly ordered.

It was a great meal, our newbie enjoyed his steak, with the peach on top, he was now an authority about steaks in the American Midwest. Our waiter? he warmed to our group when he saw how much we were enjoying the meal.

'Noo Zeeland eh, you all are a bit different, say that's a cute accent.'

'Accent? what accent? now that you mention it *you* certainly have a strong accent.'

It always throws them, Americans, when you turn the accent thing back on them.

Queue or Line? what's it to be? Well it depends what country you are in. America.

'Form a line here please.'

'Pardon me? You mean I should queue here?'

'No, stand in line, right here.'

'Yes yes I understand, you want me to queue up.'

'No I don't, this is not the hairdressers, I don't want you fiddling with your hair I want you to stand in line right here.'

A queue? is it something you do with your hair or does it mean you line up with other people?

Things are different in America.

Friday, fish day, they serve fish on Fridays. Well they serve fish every day, however, on Fridays it's a big deal, you are expected to order fish. Restaurant menus are heavy on fish on Fridays. Another Friday thing, TGIF. Thank God It's Friday. The bars are crowded, plenty of promotional activities to get you into 'my bar' on a Friday afternoon and keep you there.

Driving, they are courteous drivers in America, well most of them are. It's a trap a Kiwi can fall into, especially if you come from Auckland. I've done a lot of driving in America particularly along the west coast. It's easy, Americans are courteous and understanding. Bit of a culture shock if you come from Auckland where it's the complete opposite, in fact you need to be careful. If you drive around a place like Los Angeles the way you drive around Auckland then you will be pulled over frequently. Indicating lane changes, giving way to merging drivers, all those things we don't do in Auckland will get you into trouble in America. On the other hand if you do all the things that a good driver does in America then in Auckland you will get nowhere fast, we are shockers, nothing to be proud of.

Americans are different.

A Weather Bomb

It's approaching, a recent creation from the world of journalism, the weather bomb. Didn't happen when I was a kid, these days they pop up quite frequently. There are big ones and little ones, this is a big one. The remains of a tropical cyclone bearing down from the north. Luci, another girl, why are the big ones all girls? There's been Giselle, Alison, Wilma, Ivy. There have been a couple of boys, Gavin, and Fergus, but it seems they are generally girls, no reason, they just are, bit of male chauvinism perhaps.

I'm going to write this live. Luci has not arrived yet but she's definitely on the way. The news media, the armchair experts, all and sundry are predicting terrible things, gale force winds, torrential rain, landslides, flooding, property damage, general mayhem. Ho Hum, we've heard all this before but you must give it due cognizance, sometimes they get it right.

Luci was born way up north and rapidly deepened into a tropical cyclone, force three, that's serious stuff. Well away from us though, several days in fact, anything could happen. The boffins have this new computer and they reckon Luci will come down here and score a direct hit, really; that's serious. But we've heard it all before, usually nothing much happens, usually, but not always; sometimes they get it right and mayhem does indeed ensue.

Some years ago a tropical cyclone called Bola, hang on that's not a girls name, bit gender neutral isn't it? Whatever, the same dire warnings were thrown around, yeah right, I'm sure it will be terrible, it was. Direct hit, serious property damage, loss of life, landslides, floods; affected the country's economy. So you have to give all this talk about Luci some credibility, bit foolish if you don't.

It's day three now, three days of warnings. Beautiful outside, warm and sunny, little wind to speak of, tonight it's all going to turn to custard, the voice on the radio said so, the morning paper is full of it, apprehension is high. One source is telling us to get our household survival kit in order, household survival kit, get real, is this the complete nanny state.

A weather bomb, what is it? Well if you go along with current 'journalist speak' it can be anything from a sudden localised downpour, a severe wind squall, a big storm, or, as in this approaching one, a tropical cyclone. There's plenty of room for imaginative expression, bit like 'text spell,' that new language variation that's changing the way we communicate. Language is a living thing, I know, I read that somewhere.

Well right now I am taking the dog for a walk before the end of the world precludes such activity. It's 'nice' outside, just hope I don't get ambushed by Luci.

Back, survived the walk, dog and I are even closer mates, still a nice day. Bit cloudy, light breeze from the north, that's where it's going to come from. It's a Friday, sports clubs are cancelling weekend fixtures, the radio is issuing dire warnings.

Couple of things to do in the garden, we have a big garden, the envy of our friends and a lot of work for me. I enjoy mucking around in the garden, quite relaxing really. Won't do too much, if the pundits are right it will be a mess after the weekend anyway. Big clean up job, always is after a blow. It's the big trees, there are several big ones, attracts the birds, that's nice, but they also create a mess, particularly when the wind gets up, it looks like it's going to get right up over the weekend.

Well that's the scene. It's now Friday afternoon, nothing's changed, we're waiting for Luci.

Saturday morning, yep, it's blowing, its overcast, but no rain, no big storm, Luci's late.

Saturday evening, Lucy has arrived but being a girl she's had a change of mind. No longer a direct hit, just a slither down the coast out to the west, very windy though. The big trees are dumping small branches and all their leaves. A couple of cabbage trees have really dumped, fronds all over the lawn, real mess out there. The cushions from the outdoor furniture are flying around and here comes the rain, heavy, but not the torrential stuff we've been expecting.

Saturday night, in bed, all tucked up. The wind is howling and there's quite a bit of rain, but not quite the mayhem we've been conditioned for, but then you can never be sure, it could have been a lot worse, we could have been unprepared. Ever since Bola the authorities have been pessimistic with their forecasting for these things, I can understand that.

Sunday, still raining, no real heavy stuff though, the wind is quite strong. Luci has moved off down country but the sting in her tail is keeping us indoors. The place is a mess outside, tomorrow, Monday, will be clean up day. We have a set routine for this, do it quite often. Pick up all the debris, blow the leaves, general tidy up, the final act, mow the lawn, there now all neat and tidy again.

Down country Lucy is still spoiling things, I know, I heard it on the radio.

Monday, clean up, into it, usually takes up most of the day to restore the place to its usual pristine state, several big bags of debris, all ready for the next blow. This one was not a big blow, Luci did not quite do as the computer predicted, no direct hit, a near miss this time, but then Luci was a girl, unpredictable. A while back Gavin and Fergus did follow the computer's predictions, boys!

But, and it's a big but, remember Bola, any of these big storms has the ability to be another Bola, so never rubbish the weatherman and his computer, he could be right!

The Wind In The Walnut Tree

From my early childhood, the sound of the wind in the walnut tree, relaxing, soothing, gentle.

Sitting outside, the quiet outside, a gentle breeze, the soothing sound as it rustles the trees.

The backyard was big, half an acre, with trees, far removed from todays tiny cross leased affair, no trees, no room. Not necessarily, there are some bigger freehold bits with backyards and trees, I know, we have one. No walnut tree though, no childhood memories, well not quite, there are trees and the sound of the wind is the same, well I think it is.

My earliest memories, the tent, it featured prominently, a fixture in the back yard out under the walnut tree. My brother and I slept in that tent, outside, very healthy, far better than being indoors and always the sound of the wind in the big walnut tree that towered above it. I'll never forget it. People don't do things like that anymore, well I don't think they do, sleep outside at home, get real, that's what houses are for. They are missing out, believe me, sleeping out in the tent was just great. You can't hear the wind in the trees if you're indoors. Mind you when there's a big storm we chickened out and bolted inside. One time a big branch from the walnut tree fell on the tent during a storm, just as well we were inside, but it would have been alright, the branch missed the two camp beds, made a bit of a mess of the tent though. I bet the wind in the walnut tree that night would have been something.

Hedgehogs, know what they are? They creep around at night, you can hear them, well if you sleep in a tent, at one with nature, you can hear them, and the local cats, they can make a lot of noise staking out their territory in the wee hours. The noise of a walnut falling on the tent and when there's a bit of a blow a lot of them would fall. I used to gather them up, put them on my homemade drying rack and sell them to the dealer when they dried out, that's the ones that didn't get eaten first. There was a time when the local council declared hedgehogs a noxious animal, put a price on their heads, their noses. We took advantage of this, I won't tell you the detail, it's not nice. Mosquitoes, the one big downside to life in the tent, a real problem and no easy fix. There was a fishpond by the tent, mosquito heaven. Mum's pride and joy. If I had my way there would have been kerosine all over it but Mum loved her goldfish and they did eat mosquito larvae. Too well fed I reckon, did not eat anywhere near enough. There was a Kingfisher, Mum's sworn enemy. It would sit in the walnut tree and raid the pool. On one occasion it got just about all the goldfish. That Kingfisher got up my nose as well, it was directly responsible for the mosquito problem.

The tent featured in my life right until I left home in my teenage years. I still have a yearning for a tent, sleeping close to nature, it's the greatest. Big cities, high density housing, hotels, might as well be on Mars.

The Estuary

'Breakfast's on the table.' I'm dreaming, what the? No it's real, a voice, a real voice, you're not dreaming, *breakfast's on the table*, *get up*. It's hard, gets harder every morning, drugged with sleep, another few minutes perhaps, no, get up, *breakfast's on the table*.

It's almost a morning ritual, my lovely lady is up, doing all those morning things that women folk do first thing while I remain in dreamland blissfully unaware of all things domestic. Household chores, awakening the house, opening the curtains, *the curtains*, sunlight streams in, close the eyes tighter, reduce the brightness. I think I'm awake, try opening the eyes, yes I am awake. It's bright, sunny, the estuary right outside the bi-folds, a magnificent sight. Flat calm, not a ripple, the far side bathed in sunlight, quite a spectacle. There are variations, fog's the best. Incredible scenes when there's fog in the morning. Heavy passing showers sweeping up from the southwest when the weather turns sour can be spectacular. Very difficult getting out of bed when that happens.

Up, out of bed, life's too short to waste in bed, how many summers have you got left?

'Breakfast's on the table.' It is, right there just waiting for my attention. *'Morning dear,'* this looks so good, a mixture of fruit, cornflakes, muesli, yoghurt, disgustingly healthy, and the coffee machine whirring away on the kitchen bench. But the best bit, the estuary right outside, the big wide ranchslider frames what is a spectacular view, a picture postcard setting, right on the beach, *our cottage on the beach*. It's fascinating, an ever changing panorama out there on the estuary. It's a busy place, all sorts of boats, ferries taking working folk into the city, guess they have been up for a

while, no sleeping in there, the Waiheke ferry taking trucks and cars over to the island, yachts going out for a day on the gulf, fizz boats galore, good keen fishermen, they've been up since before dawn, got to be keen. Bit early for the foilers, the latest craze, wind foilers, kite foilers, wing foilers, everthing's on a foil. No wind this morning, could be we won't be seeing them. The kids in their P class yachts will be a bit pushed as well. Not to worry the wind's bound to get up later. The estuary will become a busy place and it's all right outside, makes breakfast really enjoyable, thank you dear for rousing me out of bed.

The Herald, it's on the table next to breakfast, the breakfast that's been lovingly prepared by my lovely lady while I've been languishing in bed struggling to come to terms with getting up. Out of bed now enjoying the beautiful morning, the ever changing estuary, life itself, how many summers?

What's that, there's something disturbing the water right outside. Eyes up from the Herald, it's misinformation anyway, how do they get away with it. Lefty journos who write all this crap, armchair commentators, trouble is people believe it, take on board their jaundiced views. Why do I subscribe? Well it's the only morning paper there is, the only paper full stop.

There's splashing, there it is, that big dorsal fin, we've seen it before, quite a few times, not just outside our cottage either but at several places around the Gulf. It's a big male Orca and he's got his pod with him, several females and some calves. They are regular visitors to the estuary, it's the stingrays, they eat them, tear their livers out, dreadful business. There are a lot of stingrays in the estuary and this pod of Orcas have got it sussed. Every six months or so they come into the estuary, right in, amongst the moored boats and anything else that's plying the waters at the time, right in on the beach. It's quite a sight and it's all there for me to observe as I have breakfast. The action gradually moves up the estuary, must be a rising tide. Smart cookies these Orcas, they'll go quite a long way up as long as the tide is rising, give the local stingray population hell, then retreat on the falling tide. We can expect them outside our place again in an hour or so.

Fascinating living on the beach, the ever changing scene out on the estuary. Been here six years now, smart move buying the old cottage, the very old rundown cottage, the *dunga*, kikuyu growing out of the roof. Our friends could not believe what we did, moving from a big comfortable well established house in suburbia, to a tiny dunga on a beach, been there longer than we've been on this earth. It's a bigger comfortable very tidy cottage now, envy of the neighbourhood. Getting it to this stage however? Yes well, they call it a *do it up,* that hardly describes the angst involved.

The reward, yes there has been a reward, a huge reward, the estuary, right outside the window, it has a calming effect quite incredible. An ever changing panorama and it's fabulous.

There's another side to the estuary, a very different side. The early morning sun has lit up the far side, it's all glistening and white, stark contrast to the dark clouds that form a backdrop to this early morning sight. Won't be long before nature destroys the uplifting sight that's been created. The black clouds will burst upon us, there'll be heavy rain, hail, thunder, lightning, the sea will get up, there will be big waves crashing onto the beach. The view out the window will change dramatically. It will not last though, never does, the scene across the estuary is ever changing, never the same, the variety is remarkable, the sun will reappear and push the black clouds away, the waves will drop and the view across the estuary will be restored but it will be different, always is, never the same, that's what makes it so fascinating, so enjoyable. I could sit and look out across the estuary for hours and never be bored, it's ever changing.

70   The Estuary

Fog, eerie foghorn sounds, misty light rain, the shape of boats barely visible, totally different panorama.

Albert McConachie's Better Day

'Albert, what about a drink after work?' It's Adele, the beautiful Adele. *Would I what!*

'Yes I'd like that, I'd like that a lot.'

Is this real, pinch yourself Albert. The lovely Adele, the girl you admire, desire, she's asking you out for a drink. Robert, his usual drinking mate, was not in today. Albert was facing the prospect of going home to his own private hell without the benefit of a couple of drinks to help him along. *Adele had asked him out,* it's usually the other way around, and Robert's always there. Couple of hours till the end of the day, Albert's mind was anywhere but on the job. *Adele has asked me out.*

'Cheers,' they're in the pub. The presence of Adele is giving Albert the warm fuzzies and he likes it, such a pleasure, such a change from what's awaiting him at home. Adele downed several drinks in quick succession, it surprised Albert, not something she usually did.

'You ok Adele?'

'No, not really.'

The warm fuzzies vanish.

'What is it Adele, what's upsetting you?'

'I'm not going to burden you with my problems, just going through a bad patch, it will pass, another drink?'

'Come on Adele what's the problem, let me help. I've got broad shoulders, feel free to cry on them.'

'You're such a sweety Albert, so understanding, it's my man, we've broken up, actually we parted some time ago, I'm just feeling a bit depressed, lonely, shouldn't be, should be happy, relieved, we were not getting on, should have parted long ago.'

Adele had been with her man for a couple of years, seemed nice enough, handsome fellow. Albert was smitten with Adele, always had been, should have met her earlier in his life but now he was married and Adele had her hunk, well she did have her hunk, but now it appears, no longer.

'What can I say Adele, it hurts me to see you unhappy, you're such a nice person, heaven knows nice people are a little thin on the ground, you don't deserve to be hurt.'

'Albert, you're the first person I've told. I've bottled it up for the past two months, putting on the happy face, pretending nothing's happened, but I need to talk and you are so understanding.'
She looked a little happier, there were the beginnings of a smile on her lovely face.

'God your beautiful.'
Albert just blurted it out, from the heart, what's happening, Adele's not attached, it's causing a strange response in Albert.

'Well thank you Albert, you're not so bad yourself, you probably don't know, but I've had a crush on you for a long time, no reason, I just like you, like you a lot, could even be more than just liking.'

Albert felt faint, dizzy, his beer glass crashes to the floor, he went deathly pale.

'Albert!'
Adele's voice was raised, people turned and looked, Adele hugged him to her, the bar attendant hurried over.

'Can I help, is he ok?'

'It's alright thanks, I'll handle it, he's just a bit faint, not a problem.'

It was a problem, a huge problem for Albert, no, that's not right, it's far from being a problem. Life had just dealt to him, one of those moments which some people, lucky people, experience sometimes. Adele just might be in love with him, the very thought bowled him completely, what were her words? *Could even be more than just liking.*

'Albert perhaps you should come home with me.'
Another wave of nausea washes over Albert, what was he hearing.

The affair developed quickly, Albert discovered real happiness, love, affection, yes Albert was in love. He had been in love before, with his wife, but it had not lasted, did not have the depth, perhaps it had not been love, just sex. It's often mistaken for love when you are young. Albert had been very young when he married. Now he was spending a lot of time at Adele's place, going home late, not talking to his wife; their estrangement intensified. It was even more unpleasant being at home. No more burnt offerings in the oven, just nothing at all. Albert needed to do something before the situation exploded, before she went right off her trolley, what to do? He needed to front up about the affair, move out. He should have moved out long ago when the marriage was on the rocks, long before the affair, now it would just add petrol to the fire. Albert agonised over just what he should do.

It was Robert, his mate at work, right out of the blue, Albert had no idea. They were in the pub, just the two of them, Albert had always enjoyed Robert's company but these days he was keen to go home with Adele after work. He had got into the pub habit during the past year or so, before he had taken up with Adele, it had been an escape mechanism, delayed going home to all that domestic misery. Now, when he thought about it, Robert was always keen on going, and staying at the pub after work, why would that be? It hit Albert like a sledgehammer.

'I'm moving out.'
This can't be, Robert was the happy guy, everybody's mate, a good guy. He was on his fourth beer when he let it out, there were tears in his eyes.

'It's over, I can't stay in that house any longer, it's sheer hell, don't know why, no reason, she just makes my life a misery, I've had it up to here.'

Albert was shocked, there had been no indication, Robert must have been going through hell, just putting on the happy front, he really was the 'happy guy.' Albert had envied him when he had been enduring his own suffering at home and now it appears it was all a front, Robert was desperately unhappy. Albert wondered if his own change of circumstances had anything to do with it, no, couldn't be, but Robert must have noticed how happy he was these days and Albert was really happy. Adele was a ray of sunshine. Albert was revelling in his new life.

'I don't know what to say Robert, I'm having trouble comprehending, you of all people! I thought I was the person who had stuffed up his life, now you tell me this.'
Robert had a haggard expression on his face and Albert felt desperately sorry for him.

'Where will you go, have you got anywhere?'
Albert's mind went back to that awful moment in his own life when he had walked out of the home where he had once been so happy, before the slow decline into domestic hell.

'Come and stay with us.'
It was an impulsive reaction but Albert really did mean it.

'We have room, Adele will understand.'
Ours was a happy household, no underlying tension.

'I'll tell her tonight, you can stay for as long as it takes, I mean it Robert.'

'I know what it's like, believe me I really do know.'

'No no I can't impose like that, you've had more than your share of this sort of crap, you don't want any more, thanks but no, I do have somewhere. It's been coming for a while. I've thought it through I've found a boarding house where I can go, I'll be ok there, out of everyone's hair. My problems are my own, I don't think people really want me crying on their shoulder.'

He looked terrible, he was hurting. Been married for quite a while, around ten years, no kids, bit like myself.

'That Cathy, she triggered it. I knocked her off in a drunken moment a couple of months ago and got found out, I reaped a whirlwind. Things had been bad for quite a while, spiralling downwards, when she found out about Cathy that was it, life became unbearable.'

Robert was letting it all out, he needed to talk and Albert was the right person, been there done that, well not quite, had not knocked off Cathy, Robert must have been really drunk!

'Guess a lot of it's my fault, I'm sure not perfect, but then she has become impossible to live with, her constant demands, the money, she spends like there's no tomorrow. I just cannot reign her in, it's become a real problem. When I try there's always a huge domestic, I just can't live like this any longer.'

They stayed on in the pub for some time, Robert definitely needed the company, Albert's going to be late home but this was serious stuff. He managed a quick call to Adele when he went to offload some of the beer.

'I'm doing some counselling, I'll be a bit late dear, going through a bit of a replay of my own life and it's not very nice, promise I'll only have a few beers.'

The big break for Albert had happened two months earlier.

'I'm moving out.'

He said it matter-of-factly to her face, he had made up his mind, was calling it quits, pulling the plug on his years of marriage. He was in love with Adele, really in love, and she was in love with him, yes it does happen. They were mature enough, been around long enough, able to recognise the emotion, the very powerful emotion, love. Albert was supremely happy, his life had taken on a whole new meaning.

Her expression did not flinch.

'Oh are you, taking off with a young bird I suppose, trading me in.'

It was going to be messy, this first exchange was not good.

'No, I've found someone. Our life here, well we don't have a life here, is finished so it would be better for both of us that we should go our separate ways.'

The atmosphere was tense.

'See you in court,' was her only response.

Oh dear, this is going to be unpleasant.

The following few months were indeed unpleasant. Albert's wife had the idea she could clean him out, leave him with very little, wrong, but some sharp talking lawyer had convinced her. She badmouthed him to anyone who would listen. Painted a picture of an unfaithful monster who had been screwing around for years, why? No reason, but then there had been no reason why their relationship had gone downhill so badly either. Albert was pretty sure that Adele was the reason for the nastiness, the badmouthing. Perhaps if he had been by himself, stayed single, it would have been different, who knows. He had noticed this reaction before when a couple separated, the moment there's another woman the nastiness starts.

Why does marriage fail, why do we split up, go our separate ways, it's a common occurrence. We were in love weren't we? What happened? Was it just sex? Could we not distinguish between the two? Were we too young? Probably. Intolerant, selfish, spoilt, too demanding, bored, had it too easy, immature, all these things perhaps. Is there a future for marriage, the trend now is marriage, divorce, then a living together partnership, 'why spoil it by getting married.'

It was an unpleasant revelation to Albert just how couples under stress can be manipulated by unscrupulous lawyers. It's pretty simple, when there's a break up it's down the middle, fifty-fifty, few exceptions. The disputes arise when a lawyer suggests to one of the parties they can get a bigger slice of the pie. The inevitable outcome, a much reduced pie, and it's still fifty-fifty. Unfortunately this is what's happening to Albert, but his life is happy, very happy, it does not seem to matter that much, it's only money, how important is money?

Finally, divorced, Albert has escaped from his domestic disaster. Adele adores him. It surprises Albert that she has adored him for so long and he had never noticed. Now his life's different, enjoyable, full of love, might even get married again, a second marriage, don't rush it, make sure. Adele had indicated that a family would make her very happy, children, she loved children, a family, and not just one.

It was not long after Albert's break up that the division manager at work called him in.

'Albert, good news, you're the new section manager, congratulations. There was competition, young Neville was right there but I think you've got the goods, the experience, I just know you will make things tick. There's a manager's car park for you as well, goes with the position, right next to the lift. You won't have to use those stairs, *those concrete stairs*, anymore,' there's a smile on his face as he says this.

Robert, they see quite a bit of him, he's single now, quite the happy bachelor, always dating, he's got a discerning eye too. *Adele is expecting,* Albert is over the moon.

Dog II

My life's turned upside down, my private domain, my absolute authority, my peace and quiet, well that's when I want peace and quiet, has gone. Suddenly it's not all me, me, me, there's another dog in the house, another Bichon, another precocious girl just like me and what's worse, she's a lot younger. My life has changed and not for the better.

Dog's now five, she needs a mate. We go out a lot and Dog is left home alone. She's such a social little creature we felt this was a bit unfair, Dog needs a mate. After some hunting around we've come up with another Bichon. Like all Bichons this one has a completely different personality. A puppy and like all puppies, everything's a game, playtime all day every day.

Go away, I don't feel like rushing around the place being chased by you. I'm mature, I no longer do things like that, can't you just settle down and chew on a sock, one of those leather belts in the clothes cupboard perhaps, a shoe, that always gets a response. I don't think they like things being chewed. Perhaps I can manage a little play, a run around, being chased by you is actually quite fun, the exercise is probably a good thing as well. Bed, a problem area, I have rights, I get first choice. You'll take what's left in the way of sleeping spots, do you understand? No? well there will be some sorting out if you don't. I'm top dog 'round here, you're number two, got it? no? bugger. I'll have to do some enforcing, how do I do that?

A major lifestyle change. We've been talking about downsizing for some time. A little old cottage, *a character home*, real estate language, old dump, my language, a '*do it upper,*' right on the water, prime location, an opportunity not to be missed. A lot of work is my take. There's going to be an auction, got to have it, just got to, *woman's talk*. We get it, now the move.

What's happening, this is not where we live, our big house is way back up the road, I know because Dad takes me for walks, I know the neighbourhood, but hang on this is a bit outside our neighbourhood, and all that water, what's that all about? And the house, it's not a house, it's a little thing, looks old. Dad said it's a cottage and it's on a beach, what's a beach? Dad said we're moving, what's moving? Moving means changing homes, why do we have to change homes? Actually it's a lot of fun, nothing is organised, we have a free run and that's what we do. A bit of growling from Dad and in no time there's this wire pen outside the back door on the lawn. Suddenly we are confined for most of the day. All sorts of people come and go. I get worn out woofing at them. My little companion seems to enjoy it and helps me woof. We are taken inside this new place in the evenings and get to sleep in the big bed. The same one that was in the big house where we used to live, why are we not still in the big house? I knew everything about that place and I liked it. Got the sleeping arrangements sorted, I've put little dog in her place and she's no longer a pest, actually I quite like her especially now that she's accepted I'm top dog. All the coming and going, tradies Dad calls them, creates a lot of woofing opportunities, I get quite worn out and have to have long sleeps during the day. It's very noisy, alterations it's called. There's a wooden thing along the front of the cottage called a veranda, then there's something called a footpath and a road in front of that, in front of that again there's a big open area called a beach, then a lot of water, very different to the big house where we used to live. It's quite nice, I think I like it. 'At the beach,' that's what Dad keeps saying. The veranda is a good place, there are always lots of people walking along the footpath, Dad says they're the health nuts, not heard that one before. A lot of them have dogs, this is great I can really give them a serious woofing, get my new mate to help, let them know this is our territory and they are intruding. Doesn't seem to make much difference though. I spend a lot of time on the veranda, patrolling Dad calls it. I'm just letting everyone know that this is my territory, buzz off!

The place is finished, the 'do it up' is now a 'done up.' Turned out rather well, lot of work. Right on the water, prime spot, swim whenever, no pool upkeep, I like that. The dogs are happy, settled into regular routines, boss dog patrols the footpath traffic from the veranda and little dog spends a lot of time sleeping on the big bed, totally different personalities. There's another small dog next door and they bark at each other through the fence, gets a bit noisy at times.

Louie, that's what dad calls him, lives next door and he, yes he's a boy dog, barks a lot, much noisier than me. We talk through the fence that's between our house and his place. I spend a lot of the day by the fence waiting for Louie to come and have a chat but he doesn't come very often and I'm disappointed so I just bark through the fence anyway. Louie came over to our place the other day and we played, he's nice, my little sister played as well. We have a big backyard at our new house and we all ran around and made lots of noise.

Our new life at the beach has settled into a pattern, different to where we used to be, living on a beach is really nice. The walks, they are different, along the beach now, very different to where we used to live.

Mary's Place

It's a big room with a large wooden table in the middle. A big black wood burning range dominates one side, always going, day and night. Aunty Mary's kitchen, engraved in my memory, just the greatest place. The taste delights conjured up in that room; to die for. Sponge cakes with whipped cream and strawberry jam, pikelets, scones, big roast dinners and fresh bread, just everything, Aunty Mary was my hero. We lived in that kitchen, big and so interesting. Butter, that was not made in the kitchen but just outside on the veranda. Daisy the cow supplied the milk, Aunt Mary separated the cream then churned the butter, it was all so interesting. Two high windows opened onto the back lawn. It was high, the back lawn, half way up the wall. And the big pantry, you could walk right in, all the jars of preserves and things that Mary was always making. The other rooms in the house were boring, well not quite all. Doug's room opened off the kitchen, that was interesting. Full of wild pig hanging from the ceiling on big hooks. The room had a lovely smell of bacon and pork. Uncle Doug was always up the hill in the bush out the back hunting, he always came back with a wild pig. He had a couple of dogs, pig dogs he called them, they helped him hunt the pigs. No wonder the pigs were wild, his two dogs would make anything wild. There was a cool store, a muslin covered box strung up in a shady tree and a huge mulberry tree in the back yard. We spent a lot of time at Aunty Mary's place, it was nice.

Memories from childhood, that magical time when everything was nice, summertime was perfect and went on forever, is life that good? does time put a rosy glow on things? Is memory selective perhaps? It must have been stormy wet and horrible sometimes, it's just I don't remember it ever being like that. Mary lived in Havelock at the head of the Sounds not far from Blenheim where we lived, we were always there, much more fun than Blenheim. Molly and Ivy lived there as well, the two cousins, they were good fun. Molly was naughty. She would climb up into the mulberry tree and be cheeky to her mum who would get wild and order her to come down. She wouldn't and aunty Mary would threaten to tell uncle Doug about it when he came home. Molly really was naughty at times, but good fun. I had an older brother, Noel, we spent a lot of time with the two cousins in Havelock. We went there in the bus, that was not nice. The road was dusty. The dust filled the inside of the bus and it always smelt of diesel. I would get sick just about every time. It was not nice that bus, that was a bad memory, but it was great when we arrived at aunty Mary's.

The kitchen opened onto a big veranda, well not a real veranda, it sort of ran through the middle of the house and had a roof on it. On one side were the boring rooms, on the other, the kitchen, Doug's room, the cousins bedroom, and the room where we slept when we visited; the good side. The boring rooms included one called a lounge, it was never used. There was a piano there that was never played, well sometimes it was, my father played it, he was very good.

Drums of diesel were stored under the mulberry tree. One day a drum leaked and the mulberry tree died, it died quite quickly and Uncle Doug chopped it down. Now Molly could not be cheeky to her mother any more. On the wall in the kitchen there was a wooden box. On one side an earpiece on a hook, on the other a crank handle. It was a telephone, a party line, a fascinating gadget. Molly had become adept at listening in on other people's telephone conversations, she was a real nosy parker. The phone would make ringing noises from time to time and you had to recognise the particular ringing sequence for Mary's place before you picked up the earpiece but Molly would always pick it up and listen in on other people. There were six houses on the party line.

The main road to Blenheim passed right in front of Mary's place, it was very dusty. The big transport trucks that operated between Nelson and Blenheim roared past the front of the house all day, they made a lot of dust. Doug had planted some big trees out front by the road and made a bank as well, it was covered with ivy and the place was called Ivy Bank, same name as cousin Ivy who lived there.

At night, when it was very still, you could hear the cars going across two bridges that were down by the top of the harbour which was out in front of Ivy Bank. The bridges were wooden and had planks on them. When the cars drove across the planks they made a rattling noise that could be heard quite clearly. We used to count to ten, which was the time it took for the cars to drive between the two bridges, if it was less than ten then they were going very fast.

One day the workmen came and tar sealed the road in front of the house, no more dust. Uncle Doug was happy when this happened, he said it had taken years to get it done. I don't know why it had taken years. When the men came they were only there for about three days and they only sealed a short piece of road right in front of the house. I don't know why they did not seal the road all the way to Blenheim. I would have liked that, but they never did. I still got sick on the bus, all the dust and the diesel fumes, I hated that bus.

Mary's house did not have a toilet, Doug said the sewerage system was years away, not in his lifetime, whatever that meant. The lavatory was an outhouse some way from the main house and there was a track across the grass to get to it. The lavatory stank, real bad, that's why it was not near the house. There was a seat with a hole in it, and all the old newspapers. You had to use them to wipe your bottom. Under the seat with the hole in it was a bin that filled up and smelled bad. Doug would pull this bin out when it was full and bury all the poo in the orchard behind the house, good for the fruit trees he said, but I never saw any fruit, Doug said it was the possums. He used to shoot the possums, they were a pest, ate all the fruit on the trees in the orchard. Doug would get a spotlight and a twenty-two rifle and go out into the orchard at night. We would hear him shooting, a lot of shots sometimes, he would come back with all these dead possums, twenty or more sometimes. He skinned them and gave the meat to the two pig dogs, rubbish meat he called it. He dried the skins on some wire frames he had made and later sold them to a fellow who bought possum skins. All the shooting made no difference to the possum numbers. He said there were hundreds of the things in the bush up the hill. We never did get any fruit from the trees in the orchard.

The toilet, we called it the dunny, was not a nice place, bad enough having to use it during the day, but at night it was a really bad experience. You had to walk along this track through the grass. It always seemed to rain at night and the grass would be wet so you would get wet. There was no light in the dunny, pitch black, it smelt worse at night. The dunny was full of spiders, big black ones and there were always strange noises at night. Going to the dunny was such an ordeal that we used to avoid it and just pee on the lawn near the house. When Mary thought we had peed on the lawn she would get angry and tell us off. We were not to be such babies and to use the toilet otherwise we would not be allowed to visit.

Havelock was at the head of Pelorus Sound. A boat did the mail run down the Sounds three times a week. We went on this boat whenever we could, it was exciting. The mail boat was the only contact with the outside world that people who lived down the sounds had, bit strange, why would you live in such an isolated place? There were a lot of big farms down the Sounds, sheep mainly. The mail boat carried everything, food, farm gear, everything that was needed. Wherever it stopped there would be a lot of activity, all sorts of things would be loaded off and on, then the boat would go to the next place where it would all be done again. The people who lived down the sounds were different, we called them 'Soundsies,' they seemed to be from a past generation. Doug said that's what isolation can do to you, whatever that meant. The mail run took all day. Just seeing the Soundsies was a lot of fun. Sometimes they gave us kids fish, blue cod usually, Mary would cook it in the kitchen, it was really nice. I loved going on the mail run.

Quite often at Christmas time we would go camping down the sounds. Dad had this big army tent and we loaded everything onto the mail boat and got dropped off in a bay down the sounds where we would camp, 'pick us up in a couple of weeks.' We used to do a lot of fishing, Dad would shoot the odd wild goat, but goat meat was not very nice, I preferred the blue cod we caught. Dad said we were living off the land like the old pioneers. I did not know what a pioneer was but we were living like them, I loved every minute of it. No dunny, just went out behind a bush, no newspaper, used a dock leaf and watch out for stinging nettle, there was a lot of it around, if it contacted your bare bottom then you would be very sore for quite a while, stinging nettle was real bad stuff.

There was a creek running through Mary's place, it was home to a lot of Koura, a small fresh water creature similar to a crayfish. My brother, Noel, liked to catch them. He would spend hours splashing around in the creek catching Koura, he would cook them up and eat the lot, bit of a foodie Noel.

All this happened a long time ago when I was a little chap, but sometimes it seems as if it was yesterday. My recollection is of a happy time. I'm sure it was. The summers were always long and hot, it never rained and everything was so nice, well almost everything, there was that bus, that was not nice, and the dunny.

Once In Ten Years

The Real Estate fellow said so, storm events, flooding, only happens once in ten years.

'It's a fact, ten years.'

'Well how come since you sold us this lovely place right on the beach we've had water, salt water, up the drive twice.'

'Well, ah there are exceptions.'

'Really.'

Exceptions all right, we've been here eighteen months and it's flooded twice, twice in eighteen months, what happened to the ten year bit?

The first time was a bit of a novelty a king tide, seawater back flowed through the stormwater drains. Flooded the street between our place and the beach, how can that be, it's a drainage system, it's not there to facilitate flooding. Well no, actually it's a design 'stuff up' and it's made a lot worse by mindless drivers speeding through the water.

'Hang on, how long has this been going on for?'

I was talking to a neighbour just after our first flooding experience.

'As long as I can remember, it floods whenever there's a king tide, well not always, atmospheric pressure's got a bit to do with it.'

'I don't recall that land agent saying anything about king tides, has anyone done anything about it?'

'Written to the Council a few times, nothing's happened, what can they do?'

'Well stop the backflow for starters, there are valves for that sort of thing.'

I thought about it for a few days. It was obvious that apart from 'bitching' the locals had done nothing. I decided to take up the cudgels. It was not rocket science, just a matter of determining 'who' in that monstrous bureaucracy called 'the Council' had the power to get things done. I got lucky, there was this one engineer who was responsible for drainage in our area, I made contact. Tongue in cheek he told me that there was no flooding problem because he had no official report about it.

'But my neighbour says he has written to Council several times.'

'That will have been filed, I do not get to see the files.'

I was gobsmacked, what goes on with the Council, it appears they just don't want to know?

'Would you like me to write to you directly.'

'Yes, I would like that, then I will have a formal complaint to act on.'

'It's on its way, with photos.'

It transpired that this engineer did know all about the problem and about the special valve that would fix it, however, because he did not have an official complaint on his desk he was powerless to act, incredulous! Things moved swiftly and inside six weeks the special valve was manufactured in Sweden, shipped to Auckland and installed. An anxious wait for the next king tide.

Two months later, low atmospheric pressure, king tide and a dry street, it works. That was not difficult, how come someone had not done this years ago? Good question and a bit of an insight into the mindset of both ratepayers and Councils. I reckon I have unilaterally raised property values in our lovely beachside suburb. Unfortunately it did not end there. The one in ten bogey was about to make itself known.

We had been in our waterfront house eighteen months, extensive renovations, complete rebuild would be a better description. Most of our 'stuff' was stored in the adjoining garage. A big storm was on the way from the north, remnants of a tropical cyclone. The authorities were warning about possible coastal inundation. We did not give this the attention that, with hindsight, we should have, big mistake! We were on an estuary, not exposed to the open ocean and there was a road and beach between us and the water. It had been blowing hard from the north for several days and a lot of water had backed up in the estuary. The atmospheric pressure was dropping and things were looking ominous, then overnight the storm hit.

A howling nor'wester, big waves, king tide and a lot of extra water in the estuary, it came right on in, across the beach, the road, and right into our place, no backflow valve was going to stop this lot. Up the drive and into the garage, our stuff, the cars. 300mm of water in the garage, a disaster. The house, an old cottage from yesteryear, had been built quite high off the ground, our forebears knew a thing or two. The garage was at ground level however. We were surrounded by water, an island. The peak of a tide only lasts an hour or so, enough time to wreak havoc. The house was okay but the garage! Everything on the garage floor was soaked and there was a lot of 'stuff' on the garage floor, and two cars. Insurance companies do not like cars that have been immersed in salt water, not even a little bit. The beer fridge, our big glass fronted depository for beer and wine, an essential item in any garage; it stood on the floor and the electrics were in the base. 300mm of salt water killed it. The garden, our beautiful garden, the source of much favourable comment from passers-by, ruined beyond salvation, plants don't like salt water.

Once in ten years, does that mean we now have ten years before nature whacks us again? It's lovely at the beach, and the neighbours? Most of them have been here a long time, reckon it's a small price to pay for such a lovely location but next time get those cars out of the place and don't have 'stuff' on the garage floor. The garden, that will occupy your time when you're not dealing with the insurance company, and it will cost, can you insure gardens?

But It's Plastic

'It's plastic!'
'Yep, sure is.'
'But it's a fence!'
'Very observant.'
'But fences are not plastic!'
'Observe my friend, a plastic fence.'

I was out the front washing our plastic fence. Our very up market, user friendly, low maintenance, high tech, plastic fence, the source of much comment and considerable disbelief. The world is a changing place, this is a plastic fence. On the beach, salt spray, a lot of salt spray when the sou'wester blows, bird poo, seabirds poo a lot, green mould, plain old dirt, not a problem, it all falls off when I go at it with the car wash suds, car wash? Yes car wash, it puts a wax coating on our lovely fence, makes it sparkle in the sunlight. No contest, get a plastic fence. Zero maintenance, no metal parts, well that's not quite true there are a lot of stainless steel screws, but they are the good ones, 316 stainless, Australian, none of this Chinese rubbish. Run a magnet over the so called stainless, revealing! Maintenance free, well that's not quite true either, it needs a wash occasionally and that's what I was doing when my neighbour accosted me. Why are you washing your fence, nobody washes their fence. Well I do, it's such a nice fence, it deserves a little love from time to time, a nice warm sudsy wash, the dirt just falls off no scrubbing required, try doing that with the standard suburban unimaginative ugly wooden affair, no contest!

'But plastic, it's not right, it's not what you make fences with!'

'Catch up my friend, it's a plastic world. Boats are plastic, cars are nearly all plastic, your money is certainly plastic, look in your wallet, what's there, plastic cards, heaps of them, any cash? that's plastic as well. Even people are becoming plastic, well almost, moulded by Facebook, only believe what social media expounds, 'must be true, it's on Facebook.'

'That's rather a cynical view of society.'

'No, a pragmatic one, plastic is taking over and an unfortunate consequence is pollution, the dreaded plastic waste. But all is not lost, we no longer cut down trees to make things, that's good for the planet. Take a look at our extension, the extra bit of house we've added, plastic.'

'What do you mean, it's weatherboard like the rest of your house.'

'Wrong, all plastic, no paint required, zero maintenance, will never show its age. all high tech plastic courtesy of DuPont in the States.'

'Really!'

'Yes really.'

Perhaps I was being harsh on my neighbour, he's a bit of a traditionalist, that's not a bad thing but anything super modern, the latest technology, well he tended to be rather critical. He was computer literate though, there was hope and he's not on Facebook. That alone was his saving grace. I'm not on Facebook either, I'm critical of the trendies addicted to it. Don't you have your own opinions, are you so desperate to be seen to conform, to be accepted, that Facebook is God, must be on it, your whole being moulded by the informed opinion found there, but aren't I always checking my e-mail, what's that tell the world? Good question but e-mail is a different creature, sure about that, or is it a generational thing, the oldies use e-mail, the youngies, Facebook. Hang on, what's this tirade got to do with my plastic fence, nothing, just thought I would vent my spleen. Facebook and its advocates get up my nose.

92   But It's Plastic

Check out the latest in plastic, just about everything's made of it and it's good plastic, far removed from the brittle yellowing stuff from yesteryear.

I'll just wash a bit more fence, cup of coffee, then I'll finish the job, my neighbour will like that, he gets to look at the fence a lot more than I do.

My Ganglion

Like something from a Stephen King story, a big 'lump thing' erupting from the back of my left hand. It's growing, is some horrific creature about to burst forth, what the hell is happening? The rest of my body? are things as they should be? have I been invaded by an alien? oh god what is happening, why me, what have I done to deserve this?

It was during a 'pee run' in the wee small hours, you know, you've been trying not to but now you have to, when I noticed this 'thing.' It's getting bigger, I'm sure it is, what is it, am I going to die? I don't want to die, I'm just a young fellow, a whole life to look forward to. I don't want a Stephen King creation to terminate it, I thought he wrote fiction, doesn't look fictional, looks very real.

Back to bed, worry worry, no more sleep. It's getting bigger, growing, god will I survive, will I be here when the sun comes up. It's only four, an eternity till dawn, I need a doctor *now*, can't wait till dawn, you'll have to wait, the world is closed at four in the morning, well around here it is. I can't stop my other hand from fiddling with it. It's getting bigger, moving, I'm sure there's movement, can't see, dark, switch the light on, can't, too scared. What if I see something, a head, eyes looking at me, these things happen in Stephen King's world, but that's fiction, this is real. I've got this thing on my hand! How long until dawn? Am I going to survive? I'm terrified, the darkness of the night makes it worse, please let the dawn arrive. I'm desperate. Out of bed, no good staying there being terrified, lights on, let's have a look.

It's a big lump, well not all that big, the light must have shrunk it, frightened the alien inside, made it retreat, where has it retreated to?

Is it going to pop out somewhere else? Morning at last, the 'thing' does not look all that threatening in the early morning sunshine, just a lump on the back of my left hand but what is it, why is it there, does it not like sunshine, is it a creature of the dark, shall I let the sun at it, scare it away.

Breakfast, not hungry, it's destroyed my appetite, going to starve me to death. What's the time, 7.30 am, when does my doctor take calls? gentlemen's hours at that place. This is serious, could be life and death, perhaps not, the 'thing' does not look so threatening now, might even be a bit smaller. I'll give him a call anyway, waste of time, definitely gentlemen's hours; eventually his nurse answers.

'Booked up to-day, perhaps tomorrow, 10am?'

'No not good enough, I've got to see him *now.*'

'Sir, calm down, what appears to be the problem?'

I describe the possibly terminal thing that has happened to me.

'Sounds like a ganglion.'

'A what?'

'Ganglion sir.'

'Is that serious?'

'No, and it can wait till tomorrow, 10am.'

'You sure?'

'Yes sir I'm sure, if you're really worried then whack it with a book, that will kill the monster.'

'What?'

She had hung up.

Ganglion, what's a ganglion, quickly, Google it, Google knows everything, there it is, all explained in considerable detail.

Whack it with a book

On Writing

I'm cleaning my teeth, electric toothbrush whirring away, great gadget, death to gingivitis. The mind is working, the ideas are proliferating willy-nilly, can I remember it all. It's a very creative time of the day, well it is in my day. The mind is super active, the challenge, get it all recorded somewhere before it's lost in an even greater avalanche of ideas. Story writing, the ideas just pop into my head, I would never have thought about that, there's this angle and that, try and remember, get it down on a scrap of paper, if the Mac's up and running, but it's not at morning teeth cleaning time, I could get it all straight onto that, bypass the piece of paper. The juices are flowing, Hemmingway said that. Don't waste the moment, the brain is working right now, take advantage, things will slow later, right now is the most creative part of the day, don't waste it. Could go on for a while, sort of feeding on itself, it may last right up to that moment when the bubble is popped.

'Dear, can you tear yourself away from that computer and do this and that for me please; now!'
End of creativity for to-day; bugger!

The writing room, Hemmingway had one upstairs, 'don't dare enter when I'm writing.' Four marriages and several affairs later he took his own life, bit of a worry. Mine is a small office off the hall, it's where I'm most comfortable writing, where the ideas keep coming, where the imagination goes into overdrive, things come to mind, quick, capture them now before they disappear back into that void and you can't recall; what was that now, damn, gone, disappeared into memory loss land.

'Yes dear I'll get to those jobs in a little while, right now I'm writing.' it's not easy.

There's another time and place that's very productive, the shower. I'm in the habit of showering late in the day when I've finished all 'those jobs.' The ideas can sometimes come thick and fast in the shower, perhaps it's the flowing water, the warmth on the top of the head, the sensual feeling of shower gel, relaxation, there's something about the shower because it happens frequently and again the challenge is to remember it all, don't lose it, get it recorded.

The bed, you're supposed to sleep when you get into bed, if only! I must be the world's worst sleeper, always have been, supposed to be bad for your health not sleeping, should I worry? When I lie on the bed and close my eyes the ideas start popping up again. The debate is, do I write it down on the piece of paper on the bedside table or will I remember it in the morning.

I love writing, it's something I've discovered in my more mature years, the more I write the more I become addicted, even had myself published, you can do it with Amazon, better than sliced bread. The publishing world hate Amazon but there's some justice there. Publishers are a pompous lot, always declining your masterpieces intimating that they're not good enough. Put some time into Amazon, it's not hard, have your very own paperback, can do an e-book as well. Read my masterpiece, it's on Kindle.

The novel or the short story? As you can see it's the short story at the moment, seems to be an easier format. The novel, every writer's dream, but it's not easy, and the time frame? It's in the back of my mind, there are some preliminary notes. The idea is to bring the novel thing to fruition, sometime, that time could be a long way off I fear, don't leave it too long though, I'm now well into my mature years, some of my friends have been falling off their perches lately, should I be worried about that?

Here we go, just thought of something, could flesh it out a bit, another short story perhaps, there are so many things to write about. That novel, it keeps receding into the future; one day perhaps!

Harry

'Dad, can we have a word?'
There was a serious edge to his voice, I detected something important was on his mind.

We live together, solo dad bringing up son. He's now twenty, a bright, well adjusted, intelligent lad, thank you God. It had been a difficult ten years for both of us. All things considered it had worked out quite well. We were best friends, that was good, but now he was feeling his oats, girls featured large in his life. I had tried hard, very hard, I liked to think I had achieved something bringing up a son all on my own. The marriage had failed a long time ago. She had taken off to Australia, did not want to be involved, wanted the money though. That had been a sore point but marriage break ups always have their bad bits. My relationship with the ex was all right, it's just that we never saw her and this was hard on Harry, he felt rejected. It had been a huge disappointment for him to handle at a tender age. Why she had chosen the path she did I could never fathom. She ran off with a fellow I didn't know, never met him. Harry had, didn't like him and that may have had a bearing on her apparent rejection. I still found it hard to accept though. A mother's bond with her child is supposed to be unbreakable, the social experts tell you this, the courts reflect it, but it's just not true, well that's been my experience. She was an arty type, quite gifted but erratic, made strange decisions, could be extraordinarily difficult at times.

Why the marriage failed, I don't know, children were a big part of it. We had been married for several years before we had Harry, there was no desire on her part to have kids, but she felt obligated, bad way to start a family. I wanted more, but no way, one was more than enough for her, not a good omen.

She was not the best mother, I don't think she had an affinity for children. This came to the fore when we split up, she did not want custody, pretty unusual and a problem for me. I like kids, but my job took me away from home a lot, it was going to be difficult. Character building, I don't need any more character. We worked it out pretty well though Harry and I, and it strengthened our relationship.

But all that's long gone, water under the bridge, lost in time. Do not want to be reminded. There were good things and not so good things, a life experience. Always learn from what life throws at you.

'Dad, I don't want to upset you and it's not that I'm not happy living at home, but I want to go flatting.'

I suspected this would be coming sooner rather than later. Up until recently I had been away a lot, Harry had enjoyed the run of the house, he was very good, quite mature for his years, there were no wild parties while Dad was away, nothing at all to upset the neighbours; there were girls of course, quite a lot of them.

'You'll get yourself into hot water Harry, girls talk to each other, believe me, I've been down that path.'

'Yes Dad, I bet you have, but about going flatting, Lauren and I want to share with another couple, we've got a place lined up in Parnell.'

Lauren was the current love of his life, a lovely girl, had my approval, but moving in together, well that's the way the world is now, certainly different to my time. I think I can get my head around it though. My working life had taken me away from home a lot, but recently I had taken an early retirement option, I was now at home full time. I think it was this that had precipitated Harry's decision to move out. I was cramping his style, I could understand that. It would also bring to a head another matter, the house.

The family home, the house we had lived in since forever, the only one I had ever owned. Built to order when I was young, happily married and mortgaged up to my ears. I still loved the place, it had it all, big and roomy, spectacular harbour views, bird feeder in a tree, lots of birds, big BBQ, lawns, gardens. Harry liked it too and that was one of the reasons it survived the marriage break up all those years ago. The usual asset split required the house to be sold, but I liked the place, so did Harry. The decision was made to hang onto it, not easy. the place had shot up in value over the years. Another huge mortgage. I repurchased half of the house that I used to own, cost me more than the original house had, kept me broke for years, but happy. Why do we do things like that, a house is a house, but in this case it was such a lovely place that I could not see us getting anything near as good again. I was concerned that if the family home became a casualty of the break up then that might have an adverse effect on Harry, he was struggling as it was.

The situation was now about to change, if Harry moved out there would just be me in a big house.

'Might have to think about selling the house.'
A shocked look, he had obviously not given that possibility a thought.

'You can't do that Dad, you just can't, get one of you girlfriends to move in.'

'Really, do you have someone in mind Harry?'

'Now come on Dad, I know you are loopy over Jeanne, she's always here, your worse than me.'

He had a point, I was very fond of Jeanne, she was a widow and a real looker, I'd known her and her husband for years, we were good friends. I'd always had a bit of a crush on her. He got the big C and died a couple of years back, since that time I've been seeing a lot of Jeanne. We enjoyed each other's company, even been on a couple of holidays together, however we both lived in our own separate houses. Harry moving out could have a profound effect on my life, did I want it all to change? Up until recently my life had been very busy and the domestic arrangements at home were just fine, but now it's all about to change. The world is a changing place. I'm always telling others this and suddenly my own world could change, change dramatically.

Why had I been single for so long, good question, it's not that I didn't enjoy female company, quite the opposite in fact. There had been numerous liaisons over the years, but nothing serious, well not in my book. Some of my female friends had become very serious, there had been problems. It had made me a bit gun shy. The constant memory of a failed marriage did little to encourage a new relationship. I would not wish it upon anyone to have to go through a break up like that. But there was Jeanne, she was different, I had strong feelings for her. The more I thought about her the stronger the feelings became, what's happening? What is Harry doing to me? Nothing, he's just brought about a focusing of the mind, a realisation of where you are, a turning point.

Lauren is a really lovely girl, she's right for Harry, she has outlasted all the others as well, a good sign. Perhaps Harry's settling down after a pretty rocky early life. There had been the boarding school in Cambridge when he was younger, it was the only answer to our domestic circumstances. I remember the principal of that school telling me he did not like the idea of people who can't make their marriages work dumping their kids onto him. That remark had hurt, but I could see where he was coming from. I made a point of getting down to Cambridge at every opportunity, going to all the school functions where parents were invited, attending the school's sports events and generally proving to that principal that Harry had not been dumped, well not by me. Harry was fifteen when I pulled him out of boarding school, it had served its purpose and he wanted to be at home, to have a normal life. Some good neighbours helped.

I trusted him enough to leave him 'home alone' and it worked, well there were a couple of hiccups, but I expected that and when he had, 'been there done that,' the arrangement worked well. Now we were at another turning point.

The house was seldom empty, Harry's friends, many of them girls, were always there, I did a lot of cooking for them all. I enjoy cooking, a skill I had acquired very quickly after the marriage break up. My cooking efforts were popular. There seemed to be considerable demand amongst Harry's friends for 'dinner at our place,' 'your Dad cooking tonight?'

'Come and have a look Dad, lunch is on me.'
He's full of surprises. trying really hard. There's a determined streak in Harry and that's a good thing. Lauren comes along and we go in to Parnell. It's an old house split into two flats, not bad considering, it'll be cold though, these old houses are not insulated, but I don't think that will be too much of a concern. Oh to be young again. I feel slightly envious, how could I raise any objection, he's twenty, your lucky he's still at home, and Lauren's lovely, he's lucky there. The two prospective flatmates arrive; I've met them before, cooked dinner for them, a couple around the same age as Harry and Lauren. There's some furniture, the bare essentials, Trade Me will be getting some business, but generally it appears to be quite a good set up.

'We have two days to decide Dad, what do you reckon?'
How could I not go along with it, this was going to happen sometime anyway, it's just that when the moment arrives it sort of knocks you off your perch a bit. Suddenly realisation, it's going to be lonely at home.

'No, I've got no objections, go for it.'

'Thanks Dad,' from Harry and Lauren gives me a big kiss, she really is a lovely girl.

'Come on Dad, lunch, there's a surprise.'

What's he got up his sleeve now?

'I took a gamble and invited Jeanne to lunch as well, she's at the restaurant. I just knew you would agree to the flat.'

Lunch was great, six of us, three couples, couples? Were Jeanne and I a couple? What have the kids done here, where is this going? We all enjoy celebratory drinks and a great meal.

'Jeanne, can we have a word, I've got something rather important to talk about.'

Leaving Home

'You're not going to be a pilot, you're just not.' Mum was quite definite; red rag to a bull.

'I will be a pilot!'

I'm not sure how the flying thing took root, but it did, and it caused a lot of disquiet in our household.

I was five when the big aeroplane appeared in the back yard, the back paddock, we called it the back yard. It was wartime and there was a big Air Force Base close by where they trained pilots. I came home from school one day, only just started school, and there it was, a huge aeroplane with two wings, one on top of the other, right there in the paddock, next to the house.

We lived on a farm near Blenheim, Dad was what they called a farm manager. There were lots of cows that Dad used to milk every day, I helped. We lived in an old house, a farm house that Mum said was a disgrace, needed a bulldozer through it, bit strange, why would she say that? There were sheep in the back yard. They would come into the house and wander about. I thought it was pretty cool having sheep wandering through the house but they used to make a mess and Mum would get angry. One day the pig got out of its pen and wandered in, that really set Mum off, I remember that. The chooks, bantams we called them, lived in the house as well, Mum got really angry with them, frequently. They pooed, and it was really messy. I stepped in some poo once, it squished up between my toes, it was yuk! I loved the farm, there were so many exciting things to do. One day I helped Dad build a huge bridge, it was down by the road, Dad called it a culvert. A big concrete pipe under the track that went up to the farm house, we covered it with lots of gravel and dirt.

Took us two whole days to build. Before we built the bridge, I liked to call it a bridge, there was a creek. The place where we crossed was called a ford. We had to pedal our bikes through the water. I could ride a bike, that's how everyone got around, on bikes. Mum was very nervous about me riding a bike, she would not let me out on the road, but I sneaked out anyway.

The big plane, how did it get there? Dad said it was an emergency landing, the engine had stopped. Bit strange, why would the engine stop before the pilot wanted it to? Anyway it had to land in our back paddock, it could not fly back to the airfield. It had frightened the sheep and they had fled, some of them had run into the house and that had frightened Mum, usually they just wandered in. I was in heaven, an aeroplane in the back yard, all mine. I climbed up and got in, there was nothing to stop me doing this. I was in the place where the pilot sat, all these instruments, levers, switches, and strange things, the pilot must be very clever, bit different to the milking shed. Where was the pilot? There were two seats in the plane, two sets of controls, two pilots, must be hard to fly if it needed two pilots. Dad said it was a Vickers Vilderbeest, what a strange name for a plane. Anyway the next morning a big truck arrived from the airfield, and a lot of men. It was a Saturday, no school, I was able to watch everything. Just as well we had built that bridge otherwise the truck would have had to use the ford and it would have got wet. It had been raining and when it rained there was more water in the creek, but now that there was the bridge it didn't matter. They took the wings off then hoisted the rest of the plane onto the truck, loaded the wings on as well, and left. Dad had to pull down part of the fence around the back paddock to let the truck in, I helped. It was very exciting. I wondered if we would be getting any more Vickers Vilderbeests landing in the back paddock.

After that I became interested in aeroplanes, I took to making model ones out of plasticine.

Dad was very clever, he could do everything. I spent a lot of time helping him around the farm. There was something called haymaking where this big machine scooped up the dry grass that had been cut and was lying in the paddock in neat rows, it turned it into big bundles called bales. We had to pick the bales up from behind the machine and load them onto a truck so they could be stored away in the barn, hard work. Then there was ditch clearing where we had to pull out all the weeds and stuff that blocked the ditches around the farm, a really messy job, I always got covered in mud. It seemed to be endless, the stuff just grew back and we would have to do it all again. One day Dad and I fixed the roof, it had been leaking. Mum freaked when she saw me up there helping Dad, they had a big argument. It was great living on the farm but Mum used to grumble a lot.

The farm's gone now, it's several years on and we have moved into town. Dad bought a shoe shop and Mum has a real house. Farming was hard in the Wairau Valley, dry, stony, burnt paddocks, nodding thistle, big gum trees, a few scrawny cows and some undernourished sheep; the land was just too poor for farming.

I was making real model aeroplanes now, flying ones, I was hooked. There was a model aeroplane club in town, I joined. Every weekend we would be flying our aeroplanes. I joined the Air Training Corps and this gave me access to all the visiting military aircraft out at the airfield by the old farm. My fascination with aeroplanes just grew like topsy. I decided I wanted to make a career in aviation, but doing what?

During a visit to the relatives in Wellington, something we did quite often, I went out to the De Havilland Aircraft Company at Rongotai and made enquiries about how I could get into aviation. I remember an elderly fellow telling me that I should go back to school, study hard, and think about joining the Air Force, that was the place to learn the business.

I was fifteen when I realised I wanted to fly, to be a pilot, didn't tell anyone though. About the same time Mum started going on about my future career, architecture or engineering, those were Mum's choices. I suspected she had found out that I wanted to be a pilot, how she could have done this I have no idea. Eventually I mentioned flying but Mum would not have a bar of it. Dad said nothing. Another couple of years and the desire to be a pilot became an obsession. I kept it to myself, Mum was totally opposed. I was saving my money, flying lessons at the aero club was the goal, Mum had no idea. Scholarship, university, that was her dream for me. Not going to happen Mum. There's going to be a bust up at some stage. Dad kept quiet. I had sounded out the Air Force. Yes I could apply for pilot training, they also drew my attention to a scheme where I could join the Royal Air Force in England right here in New Zealand, now that really appealed. I applied to join and when Mum found out there was a bust up, no way was she going to allow it. Dad entered the fray on my side, things were not good at home. When the Royal Air Force idea came up Mum went right off her trolley. I felt like some kind of monster. Why was I upsetting Mum so much, but then perhaps Mum was being a bit selfish trying to impose her wishes upon me. She seemed to want to wrap me in cotton wool, always had, anything Mum construed as risky was not allowed, must be a mum thing. I was interviewed by the Air Force, went through the selection process, and was accepted, but because I was not twenty-one parental consent was required. Dad was agreeable and Mum finally started to back down. She had perhaps realised that I really had made up my mind on a career path, it was going to happen regardless. I tried hard, really hard, to convince Mum and after a while she tearfully agreed that if that's what I wanted then all right she would give her consent, but why England? Well the RAF have a lot of real aeroplanes, the latest jets, here there's not much at all.

'But it's dangerous.' Mum's words.

'Come on Mum your sensationalising, no more dangerous than being born, birth is terminal you know,' that brought a smile. I think Mum was finally coming to terms with my career choice.

Events moved quickly. Off I went to Taieri to learn to fly Tiger Moths. I had been accepted into the RAF scheme but I had to do some flying training here before I was shipped off to England. They wanted to see if I had the 'right stuff,' was not likely to fail further down the track. Must have been ok because after a couple of months the RAF confirmed they would take me on, then disaster, absolute disaster, Dad died.

I was at Taieri deeply involved in learning to fly when I got the call. Dad had been diagnosed with terminal cancer, my whole world collapsed. I was offered the option of terminating my training and returning home to help Mum but that would probably be the end of my budding career. I was shattered, what to do? Mum phoned, she advised that Dad's desire was for me to remain at Taieri, she was agreeable to this and that's what happened. It was hard, unbelievably hard. I went home twice during the next few weeks and that made it even harder. Dad looked terrible, my hero, the one person I admired, was just wasting away. I threw myself into all that was involved at Taieri, it took my mind off Dad and I did very well on the course.

Dad died a few days before Christmas; it was the worst day of my life. I had never felt so terrible, life had lost its meaning, what was I going to do? I was supposed to be going to England in just three weeks, how could I do that, what would Mum do, everything was falling apart.

It was a while before I snapped out of it. Mum was handling everything much better than I was and surprisingly she was the one who became the tower of strength. What was planned will go ahead,

Mum was quite definite on this. The upshot was me sailing out of Wellington on a sunny January morning leaving a sad faced bunch of relatives on the wharf thinking they would never see me again. Mum was crying, she was hurting. First Dad, now me, she was alone. It was not a happy day for anyone. I was nineteen years old and I was sailing off to a totally different life.

ANZAC

ANZAC Day, an institution in New Zealand, the whole country remembers. Dawn parades, old soldiers, stories about past heroes, past deeds of valour, emotional scenes, descendants reminisce and I cannot work up any enthusiasm at all, why? Because I do not particularly want to remember war, I know what it's all about. I spent quite a few of my younger years in the military, my finger on a trigger, I never had to pull that trigger which is fortunate because if I had I would not be here, neither would you; it was a nuclear trigger.

The Cold War, the one you don't know about, the one where nobody was killed. Well that's not true but that's the public perception. The war no one wanted to start because if they did then life on earth would cease. They called it MAD, mutually assured destruction and that's exactly what it would have been, I don't particularly want to remember that.

Who does enthuse about ANZAC? A lot of people, they think it's the patriotic thing to do. People who don't have a clue what war is all about. It's become trendy and today you've got to embrace trendy things. Facebook and its clones convince you, but who puts these things on social media, do they know about war? The younger generation are into it, you cannot say a word against that, can't be a wowser, but do they know what they are being enthusiastic about?

Old soldiers feature large at ANZAC day parades. It's understandable, they want to respect their mates who did not come home from what started out as a big adventure and turned into a nightmare beyond their comprehension, death in a foreign land. For many of these old soldiers it was the dominating event in their lives, nothing else came close, they were overwhelmed by it. Emotions generated at the time have stayed with them for the rest of their lives. Those past wars were shockers, death all around, your mates killed right beside you, shell shock, shattered bodies, no let up, it drove men crazy and they never recovered. It's understandable why they turn out for ANZAC, but not all, some do not want to be reminded, it's all in the past and it's not nice, why drag up the memories?

My war was vastly different, there was no direct danger, no horror, no killing people, but the stakes were so high it's difficult to comprehend just what could have happened. I was not stuck in a trench with dead and broken bodies or trying to shelter behind something, shooting at an enemy and being shot at, people being killed, blown apart, death all around, will I survive? No indeed, my war was hurtling along in a high-speed jet right down on the deck with a nuclear weapon that would wipe out thousands, probably tens of thousands, with one press of the trigger. It did not affect me at the time, well there was a bit of a 'twitch' for a while, however, there's been no emotional toll over the years. I have come to realise just how terrible it could have been. If the Cold War had become a 'hot war' I doubt I would have survived day one, in fact there would not be many people left alive on the planet. The fire power that would have been unleashed would destroy the world several times over, MAD indeed.

I have no desire to recall this period of my life, I was part of something that could have wiped out civilisation, why would I want to remember it, glorify it?

There is another reason. I don't have any medals to wear at a parade, medals were not handed out during the Cold War. Dangerous yes, very dangerous at times, but no medals. I would feel like a fraud being amongst all those old fellows covered with medals.

Those are my reasons, my thoughts, my feelings. ANZAC Day, I sometimes wear the poppy, made in China. I feel guilty being seen in public without one, but then that's me, my war was different.

Bill & Teena Go To Europe

'Check your e-mail, I've sent you the latest from the Brays.'
We are enjoying an excellent meal at Wei Xiao Bao, our favourite restaurant, something we do on Wednesdays. The Brays are in Europe, Italy, an extended holiday in a campervan. The planning had been a major, went on for months, years. Trip of a lifetime, an expedition, a major logistics exercise. We've been hearing snippets for months about all that's involved. Bill's very thorough, he's also a car buff hence the motor home, not just any old motor home, not Bill, this one's flash, all the latest gismos, a travelling hotel. From the bits of information picked up on successive Wednesdays I've deduced that the grand plan is to 'do' Italy, France and Germany, and generally immerse themselves in all things European, I'm envious,

'Need someone to carry your bag?'

They have created this 'blog,' you know one of those social media inventions that allows you to tell the world what you are up to, a phenomenon that seems to have suddenly become a necessary part of our social structure. This one is conservative, private, there's a password. Bill and Teena are 'conservative,' not 'in your face.' Some of the social networking mediums are very much 'in your face,' I mean who really is interested in what you had for breakfast, or what the cat did, or that your left eyebrow is itchy again, no passwords, tell the world, riveting stuff.

The e-mail has come from Keith, Bill's conduit into our small group, we dine every Wednesday evening, 'good meal night.' Nearly always Asian. We have our favourites, our preferred menus. Been doing it since forever, sort of a throwback, an old form of social networking. We actually get together and talk, social intercourse, no electronic gadgets, just a few social skills like the ability to converse, discuss, use your voice, an endangered activity these days, generation gap.

The Brays are having a good time, photographs, tales about fascinating places, a lot of eating. They have a daughter with a handsome Italian boyfriend, fiancé now, they're in Italy as well. The prospective in-laws, they feature large on the blog at the moment and the sun seems to be shining all the time and everything appears to be warm and fuzzy. Winter setting in here, wet and windy, the temperature's heading south.

'Next.' A small red prompt in the centre of the screen, right in amongst some page binding stuff that makes it difficult to see. Ready made commercial blog, pay your money and you can 'blog.' 'Here's a great blog site, just for you,' pity about the prompt. Next brings up some more pictures of the happy travellers, more documentary about the great places they are visiting. There's something about getting offside with the law and having to make a contribution to the state. Not like the Brays, must have been entrapment. Been gone a few weeks now, the table talk is about their coming home, but it seems they've only just left. Our happy group of diners has only been deprived of their company for a few Wednesdays, does time flash by that quickly?

Another communication from Keith, check your e-mail, the latest. More restaurants, spectacular scenery, a cathedral, more clicking on that little red next hiding in the binding. Now it's Rome, three coins in a fountain, the Sistine Chapel, the Vatican, an attempt on Teena's handbag, what? Teena mugged, never! The mind expanding experience of travelling, way out of your comfort zone, strange and different behaviours, perhaps it's the travellers who are strange and different, depends on your point of view, your position in life, your location on the planet. Italy's 'done' next it's Germany, we will have to wait a bit for the next enthralling missive from the travellers. Pass the prawns please and the salt and pepper squid, bit peckish tonight, lunch was rather skimpy.

Disaster, total disaster. I was tidying up, removing unnecessary files from the computer, speed it up, it's getting slow, old, cluttered, get rid of some of the junk. Eh, that was not junk, some of those unnecessary files were actually an integral part of the e-mail programme. Big mistake, irreversible mistake, blank e-mail screen, no e-mail, *no e-mail*, but I can't exist without e-mail. A lot of desperate fumbling with the intricacies of a modern, well perhaps not that modern, computer, no joy, blank screen. What to do, whatever it is, do it quickly or you will drop off the planet. It never used to be like this, I have lived a long and fulfilling life without e-mail, how come I am looking at a life stopping situation just because I can't get e-mail, the world is a changing place but this is ridiculous. Well no it's not ridiculous, that's the way it is now and if you want to continue in society you had better get your e-mail up and running again, pronto.

Decision time, my state of the art computer, hang on you've had it eight years, it's no longer state of the art, bordering on antique is more accurate, replacement time, but I can't afford a replacement, well you're going to have to!

Replacement, I've been thinking about it for quite a while. Every time my friendly computer tells me that free updates are available, all you have to do is 'this and that' and when I do 'this and that' I get a slap in the face, the words, the very rude words, on the screen tell me that my operating system is too old to accept the latest updates. What it does not say, but certainly infers, 'for god's sake get a decent computer.' Well it seems crunch day has arrived, I've got to do something, now.

I've had my eye on the one I want, the very latest in computer technology, a giant leap into the future. It'll be good for years, and future proof, hang on, that's what the man said last time and look at the angst it's causing me right now. The one I've got my eye on is the answer but it's not cheap, seriously good though and in this modern world you just have to have a good computer. The things rule our lives, they really do, I mean look at me right now, no e-mail and I'm distraught. Ok, decision made, action. I check the suppliers and bingo, my lucky day, there it is, my dream computer, and it's on sale, *on sale,* those ones are never on sale, well yes they are, it says so right here. Better get down there and check, seems a bit unusual, could be lucky. Yep, it's for real, on sale.

It's installed, up and running, but that blog, that insight into the happy travellers European adventures, gone, irrecoverable, but hang on the Brays are home in a couple of days, get it all direct, word of mouth.

I guess this tale, my first encounter with a *blog,* will end in Italy, the German bit, and the homecoming is not there. Caution, word of warning, don't go erasing those mysterious files you know nothing about.

Losing A Tooth

Ahhh, pain, excruciating pain, toothache, real headache stuff, what to do? Well check your credit card limit and take yourself off to the dentist. I remember, he's along on 'what's a name street,' I went there once several years ago. A school dental nurse's filling from yesteryear had failed. That cost big time, root canal, capping, two visits, zillion dollars, never been back, can't afford to, now I have to, have to go back. Wonder if they're still there? Could just ignore it, yeah right, how much pain can you suffer, it's not going to go away, probably get worse, bugger, little choice, where's that phone number. Ring, ring, hang on that's not the normal ring tone.

'This number has been disconnected, please consult your phone book for the correct number.'

Bugger, what was the name of that dentist? Yes I remember, well I think I remember. Google it, yes there they are, different address, different number. I wonder if they're the same crowd, would have thought they'd keep the same number.

'Yes sir we can book you in for Thursday, 11.30 in the morning.'

'But that's three days away, this tooth is killing me.'

'We're very busy sir, Thursday's the earliest we can fit you in.'

Three days of suffering, Panadol, lots of Panadol, how much is this going to cost? Dentists are very wealthy, aren't they? captive market, charge whatever the market will stand, everyone does these days, it's just the way things are.

'Mr Mangin, we've found your records, not seen you for a while.'

'Well nothing's gone wrong, no need.'

'That's not a good idea you should have regular check ups, dental hygiene is very important.'

'I'm a pensioner, can't afford it.'

That killed the conversation, perhaps drew her attention to the exorbitant cost of going to the dentist.

'Well now John Green, whose patient you were, is no longer with us so we will put you with Jessica Thorn, is that alright with you?'

What an odd question, who the hell is Jessica Thorn, am I supposed to have an opinion based on zero knowledge. Perhaps I should draw her attention to the stupidity of her question.

'I have no idea, who is Jessica Thorn?'

'Oh, she's recently joined us from Otago University, very bright young girl.'

That means she's fresh out of dental school and they want to palm off some of their patients to her. I'm not exactly a patient of high standing so I get Jessica. Ok, give the girl a chance, at least she'll be up with the state of play unlike some of the 'ancients' in the business, might even be a pleasant surprise.

'Hello Jessica, I'm Rex and I've got the mother of all toothaches.'

'Well now Rex tell me a bit more about it.'

Jessica is an attractive brunette, early twenties, nice figure, looks like she might be a gym bunny, getting good vibes, might have got lucky here.

'Well Jessica a couple of weeks ago a filling fell out. An old school dental nurse job, pork crackling, must have broken it. There were two pieces of old amalgam. I ignored it at the time, that's what elderly men do until suddenly, toothache, so here I am.'

'Right let's have a look.'

Jessica spends some time investigating. I was impressed with her businesslike approach, perhaps I've found a good dentist.

'Rex this is what I've found. A large filling has come out and exposed the nerve end hence the pain. I think the nerve has deteriorated as well, partly age, partly because it's been exposed for a while, the fix, root canal and capping.'

'Ah, what's plan B.'

'Extraction.'

'Tell me about the costs involved Jessica.'

'Well a root canal will be around $450 to $500 and a cap, another $700 plus, all up say $1200 plus.'

'And plan B.'

'$250.'

'Plan B please Jessica.'

'Well hang on a bit Rex, that means you lose the tooth, that's not necessary, we can save this one.'

'Look at it this way Jessica. The tooth is at the side, you can't see it from the front, can't see it when I smile, so aesthetically it doesn't matter. The cost, $1200 plus, or $250. I'm a pensioner, cost is a big consideration.'

'But you just don't get rid of a tooth because of the cost, it's part of you, you have to keep it.'

The keen young girl was having trouble comprehending just where I was coming from so I'll hit her with this.

'Jessica I'm four score years plus six, several years beyond my use by, spending up big on teeth is not a good investment. How many years use am I going to get from a nice new cap? It's at the back, no one can see it, sooner have the $1000.'

I felt bad, Jessica could not comprehend my logic. I found my decision a little different as well. Up until this moment I would have gone for the 'keep the tooth option' but suddenly, realization, what's the point of spending that sort of money for what? I don't need the tooth, you can't see it and how long am I going to have to live with this terrible loss.

'Pull it out Jessica.'

'You absolutely sure about this.'

'Absolutely, tell me how do you do it these day, big pair of pliers?'

'Very different now, I'll slice it into three sections vertically and remove each piece separately, a little local anaesthetic and you won't feel a thing.'

She did, I was impressed, Jessica was good. I've found myself a dentist, someone who will stick around for as long as I will be needing a dentist.

The Garage

The garage, it's for the family car right? wrong. Sure the car's in there sometimes, keeps it clean, out of the weather, the rain, protected from deterioration, rust, corrosion, but a lot of the time its outside in the drive because Dad's doing something in the garage. It's his workshop, the place where he keeps his tools, assorted junk. Where the beer fridge is, the old broken boat trailer, all sorts of stuff that we don't use but might need one day. 'Don't throw it away just yet,' you said that five years ago. Every house has one, a garage. It starts life as a neat and tidy place where the car lives. Mum said we will keep it tidy not let it get cluttered up with junk. Well it's nice to have an aim in life, a goal to achieve, something you have decided to do and not get sidetracked, follow through, make it happen. What went wrong? Well it's a garage, that's what happens to garages, all garages? No, not your garage? Sure about that, had a look lately, a serious look, not a blinkered fixed straight ahead gaze when you go through the garage? 'Where's the car?' It's in there, somewhere. Get it out, you have to get it out, there's the grocery shopping, it's Tuesday, discount day, need the car. It's usually parked in the drive but today it's in the garage; just. Careful, don't scrape anything as you extract it from all the stuff stacked around it. Difficult making enough space to open the driver's door. There will have to be a clean out soon, this is ridiculous, the garage needs a good sorting out. It won't happen because it never happens with garages, where will we put all the stuff? How about getting rid of it! No not that, I might need it, yeah right you said that five years ago and you've not touched it since, but I might!

It's human nature, the junk accumulates as long as there's space available, jam it all in, it's all good stuff!

We're moving, downsizing, smaller house, there is a garage, small, room for the car only. 'But where are we going to store *our* stuff?' 'You're not going to store *your* stuff anywhere you're going to get rid of it,' 'but?' 'but nothing, it's all got to go.' Perhaps a storage place, you know one of those places where you can store stuff. Why, pay good money to hang on to stuff that you've never used for years, will never use again, the dump's the place. Perhaps Trade Me first then the dump. But? but nothing, it's all going! Could start with putting some of it out on the kerb, it's amazing what people will take, easy option, let's start right now! No, wait a bit, don't be so hasty. No nothing, we're going to start right now, not in five years time we're moving, we've got four weeks to downsize starting now. The new house is half the size of this one and the garage is small. We're over the big house thing, get into the garage and start sorting, there's not much time, 'yes dear.'

It's heartbreaking, can't bear to part with it, never use it but I like it, used to use it but then the better model came along and of course I had to have it. Keep the old one though, you never know, I could use it again, one day, just put it up here in the garage. There seem to be a lot of things in the garage that have been superseded by the much more advanced model but I'm attached to the old one and there is a space up here where I can store it. Store it for what? why? think you might use it again one day? get real you will never use it again it's now just a piece of useless junk, probably dosen't work anyhow, out it goes. Try the kerb, someone will take it, surprising what some people will take, ok, the kerb it is.

Thirty minutes later, I'll just go down the drive and get the mail. It's gone, I only put it out half an hour ago and it's gone, someone wanted it, I should have kept it, someone could see the value in it, a little part of me has been stolen. I'd had it for forty years and now it's gone, who's the new owner? what will they do with it? will it still work? should have kept it.

The Piano

Imagine an old piano, a very old ordinary upright piano, a piano that's given the world beautiful music during its long life. Probably the proud possession of someone who acquired it brand new, treasured it, loved it, made beautiful music with it, owned it their entire life; then they died.

'What do we do with grandpop's old piano, must be sixty if it's a day, any of you want it?'

'Yes, I'll have it,' and the piano has a new loving owner.

Well it was loved for the first year then the novelty wore thin, interest waned. The modern world held too many other more exciting attractions. It was not played, years passed, the piano languished in a back room, a cold musty back room.

'We should get rid of this old piano, it's just taking up space.'

'No, can't do that, it was grandpa's, he loved it, the idea was for me to look after it.'

'Well are you? looks pretty sad to me, get rid of it.'

'No, not yet, I'm going to start playing it again, not many people play the piano these days.'

'Yeah right, I'm sure you are.'

I did, there was renewed interest in piano playing but age, inattention, and that cold damp back room had killed its voice, reduced it to a sort of tuneless clunking of keys on cardboard sound, call the tuner.

'Possible, it's pretty far gone but nothing's impossible, will cost you.'

'How much?'

'Can't say until I get the thing apart, there's mould and a bit of rust, the strings will need to be replaced but it's a good piano, *was* a good piano. How come it's in this sad state?'

'Oh well you know, lack of interest, clutter, stuff you don't get rid of until you have to move house, but I would like to start playing again, how much do you think?'

'I'd say around the five hundred mark but you would have a good piano again, this model is a good one, worth restoring.'

'Right do it.'

And so the piano had a new lease of life, beautifully restored and moved to the front room, now a featured piece of furniture. I brushed up my playing ability, you never really lose the touch. We had lovely piano music in the house, even the neighbours commented how lovely it was to hear piano music wafting out of our house, a rarity in this modern world of long haired guitar strumming youth.

And so it was. The piano lasted for another ten years then disaster, family circumstances changed dramatically, there was no longer room for the piano.

'We'll take it down to the auction rooms, might get a bob for it.'
We did, end of an era, hope grandad's ghost does not notice.

Officers Mess Christmas Island Central Pacific, Operation Grapple, Britain's nuclear testing programme.

'Sir, there's a truck here with a piano for the mess, just arrived on the supply ship, where would you like it placed?'

'A piano, did not know a piano was coming, could be a welcome addition to the mess, how about over here by the bar.'

'Right sir, I'll get right onto it.'

And so the Officers Mess on Christmas Island, way out in the middle of the Pacific, had a piano, grandpop's old piano. I wonder what the future holds, not the greatest environment for a fine musical instrument like a piano. Not wrong, it was a terrible environment. It did get played. A few of the officers who had been forced to learn by domineering mothers still had the touch. Once you can play a piano it never leaves you and when you have grown up a bit you're glad mother forced you to learn. The piano was played, frequently, early evening, but unfortunately as evening turned to night, and the beer intake increased, things deteriorated and the piano became a place where you parked your beer glass, your still partly full beer glass, while something else occupied your attention. It kept happening, the piano was constantly having beer spilled over it and this did nothing for what had been a lovely tone. There was always the chap who reckoned he could tune it. Unfortunately for grandpop's old piano this usually happened late in the evening and the tuner's fiddling did nothing for the piano's tone. It got to the stage where the piano players lost interest, it sounded so bloody awful that nobody bothered to play it anymore. The poor thing just stood there in a corner by the bar, something to park your beer glass on, something to spill your beer over, a terrible fate to befall what had been such a fine musical instrument, the source of much pleasure to many people over the years. The island climate, the coral sand, frequent beer spills; deterioration was rapid, then the ultimate disaster, the death of the piano.

It happened late one evening after a particularly drunken session. Someone decided that the useless piano in the corner, the piano that sounded so bloody awful, the piano that nobody played anymore, should be disposed of. A cruel and ill-considered decision, but it was probably the beer talking. There was no knight in shining armour to intervene for grandpop, no piano saviour came forward. The poor thing's fate was sealed. It was carted down to the beach and unceremoniously tossed into the tide, good riddance, the thing was just cluttering up the bar.

Next morning, 'oh shit,' too late, far too late. The surf had reduced grandpop's pride and joy to matchwood. Who did this? Accusations flew about, 'ah, don't remember, don't remember anything, bit drunk last night.'

And so the matter was put to rest. Grandpop's fine old piano became part of the debris along the high tide mark on a remote coral atoll out in the middle of the Pacific.

Rest in peace.

Oh Shit Moments

You know, those times in your life that cause you to use that colourful expletive, those two words that relieve that maddening emotion when realisation strikes home, you've got it wrong, stuffed it up, made a mistake.

'Oh Shit,' relief, now I feel much better.

Discovering a bill in the pile of paper littering your desk. On examination you discover that its *please pay by* date has been and gone, then further discovering in the fine print that a 10% penalty applies if not paid by the due date. This will probably elicit a milder form of self rebuke, *bugger.* Further perusal of the defaulting account draws your attention to the fact that the sum owing is rather large and there's a note stating that this account has a history of being overdue and if this state of affairs is to continue then we will have to consider reviewing your credit worthiness. Your response will probably escalate to *'Oh Shit.'*

The intensity and emotion of the expletive used on a particular occasion will very much depend on the real or imagined severity of the situation, for instance.

Hammering in a nail, and you miss the nail. The Barry Crump expletive *bugger* is probably appropriate, however, if you hit your finger in the process then it's a *'shit,'* probably quite loud and quite involuntary. If the misfortune with the hammer escalates and it becomes a severe blow to a finger with skin damage and blood then it's escalates all the way to the most powerful and vulgar of them all, invariably expressed in a loud voice, *'FUCK.'*

Are these expressions acceptable? Depends who you ask. In the building industry they are common along with a lot of other words that are not generally considered acceptable but then bad language is endemic in the building business. Just stop and listen at any building site.

'Bugger' has won acceptance in society mainly as a result of the Barry Crump commercials of yesteryear but the more expressive terms that we use quite involuntarily when things go wrong are generally frowned upon. The ultimate expression of frustration and anger the *F* word is a no no, however, it has become fashionable to use it to add impact and shock value to a statement.

Escalation: - *bugger – shit – f---!*

The Tent

Childhood memories, the tent. We lived in a tent. Not all the time, there was a house. Mum and Dad lived in the house, us kids, the tent. A nice tent, wooden floor, low wooden wall, two beds, me and my brother. The tent was under a big tree. During the night if it was windy the tree made noises, nice noises, and the tent flapped about a bit. If it rained as well some rain would blow inside the tent but most times it stayed dry. Mum said sleeping out in the tent was very healthy. During my childhood years I slept in the tent, not all the time though, Dad took it down during the winter. Winter could be cold, frosts, we moved inside during the cold months.

When I was young we moved house several times, the tent always followed. The first thing Dad did after a move was to build a wooden floor with a low wall around it then up went the tent. There was a second tent that went over the top called a fly, that ensured the inside of the tent would be dry when it rained. There was a problem though sleeping in a tent when I wanted to pee. Mum said I had to go to the toilet in the house, this meant going across the lawn. There was always a lawn and it would always be wet. My feet would get wet and cold so I just peed out through the opening at the front of the tent onto the grass. Mum got angry whenever she suspected I had been doing this, which was all the time. She could tell because the grass in front of the tent never did very well, it kept dying off, Mum said it was because I had been peeing on it.

There was one place called Whites Farm. Dad was the farm manager. The tent was some distance from the house under some big macrocarpa trees. It was a good spot, plenty of shelter. A lot of quail used to hang around the tent, I think they wanted us to feed them.

One morning there was a loud bang. I could hear something hitting the canvas of the tent then I heard Mum going ballistic up in the house. What's up? what's happened? There were people staying with Mum and Dad at the house and one of these guests, a young fellow, had spotted the quail and taken a shot with a small bore shotgun, he called it a 410. A couple of the quail were killed and several of the pellets from the shotgun had hit the tent, it was this that sent Mum right off her trolley, I don't think I will ever forget that.

The tent continued into my adolescent years. When my older brother left home I was alone in the tent, it was nice, part of my life. I lived in a tent at home, and I liked it. Sleeping inside was a bore, ok during the winter when the tent got a bit cold, otherwise, the tent every time. I was eighteen when I left home, joined the Air Force, and that was the end of the tent. I think dad pulled it down, don't know what happened to it. I've often thought about the tent, how much I enjoyed sleeping out. I guess I spent most of my young life sleeping in that tent, different!

Albert McConachie

Five years have passed since that terrible period in Albert's life. There's a son, Matt. Adele and Albert are still madly in love. There was a big wedding. Life's been kind, a timely lotto win, a good one, how lucky can you get. Robert, their good friend, found another life partner after a couple of years playing the field, he was much sought after by the ladies, good guy Robert, this time he's found the right one.

The lotto win helped restore Albert and Adele's finances to respectability after the messy divorce. Now they live in a little old cottage on a beach, a very comfortable little old cottage. Albert's ex went off to Australia. He did hear she married again, must have been an Australian fellow, *good luck.* Reminded him of that perceptive observation by a former New Zealand Prime Minister about New Zealanders going to Australia. *Good thing, raises the IQ of both countries.*

They see a lot of Robert these days, their friendship has strengthened over the years since that bad time, holidaying together, cruises. Robert's lady, Tammy, his wife now, gets on well with Adele, we make a happy foursome. The work scene's improved, really improved. Albert's now the number two man in the company, substantial salary, late model company car and a spot in the executive car park far removed from that concrete staircase. Won't be long before the directors offer him the top job, he's 'had the word.' Bit of headhunting going on, there have been offers, something the directors are aware of, can only be good for Albert. Adele gave away working not long after the wedding when she fell pregnant, these days she's an up and coming author. Life revolves around her, their friends and all their children, seem to be quite a lot.

A lively social scene and quite a bit of holidaying abroad a lot of it accompanying Albert on his frequent business trips. Adele's writing is developing, she's self publishing on Amazon, e-books and paper backs. It was children's books at first but that's a crowded field, now she's branched out, writing short stories, lets her fertile imagination run riot. There have been several collections, all well received, people are starting to ask for her. If this continues the established publishers could come calling. Fat chance, they're a pompous lot and they hate Amazon. It will be a novel next, every writer's dream but that's a long term thing, not easy. There was one encouraging sign during a business trip to Germany with Albert. They went along to the Frankfurt Book Fair, the world's biggest, Adele was pleasantly surprised to discover that her name, Adele McConachie, was known, people in the industry do take notice of what's published on Amazon.

It started with mild morning sickness, Adele you're pregnant, but she wasn't, just a bit crook in the mornings, it will pass, don't worry about it, but it persisted. Eventually it was the doctor but he could not find anything conclusive, then it just went away.

Twelve months on, Albert was promoted into the top job, Adele's novel was well underway, young Matt started school, their lives were pretty full on. Then it started again, the morning sickness, along to the doctor and guess what, this time *you are pregnant*, life was complete. The morning sickness became severe, bit of a worry, the doctor again, no it's just the pregnancy. A couple of months on and it was no better, perhaps a second opinion. There is this fellow in the city who is highly recommended, let's try him.

'*Hmm, something's not quite right here perhaps a body scan.*' The scan did not show anything untoward, bit of a mystery, *must* be the pregnancy. Another month and there's some vomiting, back to the doctor, another scan and this time there's a shadow on the pancreas, what does it mean? Well it could be one of several things, we'll monitor it for a while. You're five months into a pregnancy, need to give that all our attention. Not a very satisfactory state of affairs and Albert was starting to worry, worry a lot. Robert and Tammy were very good, plenty of support, then one morning Adele collapses and is rushed to hospital, lots of tests, a few anxious days of waiting, then an awful result, Adele has pancreatic cancer.

It was a terrible time for Albert, he was camped at the hospital. Adele was not getting any better, the baby? At this stage there's nothing we can do, it's five months along and it limits what we can do in the way of treatment. Then early one morning Adele took a really bad turn for the worse and was rushed into intensive care. It was around eleven in the morning when the doctor sought him out.

'I'm so so sorry but I have to tell you, it's terminal' – Albert's life imploded.

About the Author

Rex Mangin lives with his partner Lynne in a cottage on a beach in Auckland, New Zealand. He is retired from a lifetime of flying and spends his days fishing, travelling, and writing.

Books By Rex Mangin

These books by Rex Mangin are available as paperbacks and at all e-book outlets worldwide.

Flying The Pacific (a memoir)

After several years in NATO's Second Tactical Air Force on the front line of the Cold War in Germany the author returned to his native New Zealand and joined TEAL, Tasman Empire Airways. During a thirty year career with the airline he was part of the enormous expansion into the present day Air New Zealand. He flew everything from the jet prop Electra to the 747-400. The Pacific, the Orient, America, and during the later part of his career, all the way to Europe. It was not a simple process however, there was a lot of angst and heartache.

This book is not just about flying, it includes everything else that's involved in an airline pilot's life, the travel, the 'holiday' stopovers, living abroad, interesting experiences, some of them very interesting, the stresses and pressures, the rewards, it's a rather unique lifestyle.

Here's a sample of the first chapter.

Joining TEAL

'Got the checkerboard?'

'Yep, got it,' replies the co-pilot.

'Height ok?' I ask.

'Yep, looking good.'

'Ok when that tall building with the mast over on the right is abeam we'll turn.'

'Yep it's coming up now.'

'That wind's picked up, better turn a fraction earlier,' the co-pilot offers.

'Yep, thanks.'

'Right; go now.'

We are flying a DC8, it's Hong Kong's notorious checkerboard approach at the old Kai Tak airport. I bank the big jet steeply to the right and peer out looking for the runway, there it is, right on cue. It's a murky evening, there's a strong crosswind blowing us right into the checkerboard, it's bumpy and we're in amongst the tall buildings. This approach is one of the more challenging things in aviation, not for the faint hearted. There's a stiff southerly requiring the use of runway 13, the south easterly one and that necessitates the famous checkerboard approach, the one the passengers love, the one that takes you right in amongst the tall buildings. The downside is that when this approach is required there's always a stiff crosswind on the runway. We complete the turn onto finals, assess the crosswind, kick in some rudder, and prepare for the actual touchdown still with quite a bit of drift on. Just before the wheels make contact I kick it straight; the touchdown is quite smooth. Hold the wing down, careful with the reverse that wind is strong. We decelerate and turn off the runway; another adrenaline fuelled Hong Kong arrival. How come I'm doing this? I'm 32 years of age and this is one of aviation's more difficult places to be flying and in a big jet full of people. It's quite a story.

Cold War Warrior
(a memoir)

A true story about a young lad who grew up in Blenheim, New Zealand, during the 1940s and early 50s. He developed an insatiable passion for flying, travelled to England and became a pilot in the Royal Air Force. He soon found himself involved in the United Kingdom's nuclear testing programme in the Pacific. This took him around the world and in just a few short years he found himself on the front line of the Cold War in Germany.

If things had turned ugly this young Kiwi, along with others, was going to unleash nuclear mayhem on Europe and would no doubt have perished in the process. This is his story.

Early Days

'Ok Harry, here we go.' I nosed the big Canberra over and headed for the ground in a steep dive, at about 600 feet with the target firmly in the gun sight I squeezed the trigger. Four 20mm Hispano cannons burst into life and sent a shudder through the aircraft, I could see the shells shredding the canvas target on the ground. When we were ridiculously close I stopped firing, pulled up

hard, and climbed away. Harry, my navigator, was jammed up in the nose cone, he must have been terrified, again! We were at a live firing range in the old West Germany practising air to ground gunnery, I was having a ball, Harry was not! How did I come to be doing this?

Well I was a front line jet jock in the Royal Air Force, actually I was in NATO's Second Tactical Air Force in Germany, how did I get to be there? it's a long story.

In our cottage on a beach in Auckland, amongst all the wine glasses, there's a copper tankard, it's lined with silver and looks old and tarnished. There are some words engraved on it. *IN HAZY MEMORY OF SALISBURY SOUTHERN RHODESIA JUNE 1962.* On closer inspection the engraving's a bit rough, the Os look like Ds however the quality of the copper, and the silver lining, appears to be surprisingly good. This tankard is a constant reminder to me about the early part of my life, the part that now seems so very far away, when I was involved in the Cold War in Europe. On occasions I ask myself, did all that really happen?

Was that me thundering around Germany in a jet, right down on the deck, eyeballing the East Germans? Was it me out in the Libyan desert amongst the flies, the sand, the heat and the sweat, trying to toss a bomb onto a target from very low level? Did I really shoot up the Larnaca range out in Cyprus with those big 20mm cannons? Did I really fly around those Norwegian Fjords in all that murk, ice and snow? That gun running business in Tunisia, did that actually happen? Was that me flying over the vastness of East Africa, the endless deserts of the Sudan? Did I do that sabre-rattling for Queen and Country in Central Africa? Was I really involved in that nuclear testing in the Pacific in the 1950s? Did I really wander around East Berlin at the height of the Cold War? Yes I did, it was all part of my Big OE, let me explain.

Mercenary (a novel)

Rex Macare, fresh out of the military, a highly qualified pilot, his apprenticeship's finished, now he wants the real money. His quest leads to the mysterious Mr Roberts who makes him an offer too good to refuse. He meets, and falls in love, with the beautiful Kate, a high end fashion model. He soon finds himself immersed in a whole new world. A heady mix of big money, huge money, dangerous flying, high end fashion, and unbridled sex. It does not last.

The story is set around the world, the South Seas, Vietnam, Paris, Algeria, Australia, and the DDR, the German Democratic Republic, the old East Germany.

It's a fast moving story that I'm sure you will enjoy.

Mr Roberts

Bzzzz, I press the doorbell, 'Monsieur Robier?' no response, I knock, 'Monsieur Robier?' still no response, have I made a mistake. I'm sure it was two this afternoon, room 202. I push the door, it swings open and I recoil in horror. The place is a charnel house, blood everywhere. There's a body on the floor, throat slashed open, I feel faint, want to throw up, it's worse than a horror movie. I look closer. The body has been mutilated, clothing torn open, blood all over the place, it's Monsieur Robier. There's something on his chest, a note.

Rentrez chez vous Monsieur Rex, ne plaisante pas avec nous.

Go home Mister Rex, don't mess with us.

French, English, my name, it's meant for me, shit! There's something else, his genitals have been torn off and stuffed into his mouth, the FLN's brutal calling card.

Carrie Gray
(a novel)

A young girl leaves New Zealand for Europe, the big OE. She goes alone, wants to do her own thing, unrestricted by others, experience everything. A skilled boaty, she wants to crew on a superyacht; she disappears. Her boyfriend, Michael, becomes concerned at the sudden lack of communication and sets off to find her; he disappears.

Michael's father Frank, a retired detective, becomes alarmed and sets off to find them both. He discovers a frightening underworld of drug smuggling, murder, and prostitution, dominated by several powerful families. It's devouvred these two youngsters from far off New Zealand.

A fast moving story of romance, adventure, and danger set in Paris, Athens, and Istanbul, and spills out into the Pacific.

Infidelity Gun Running & Other Tales

Fourteen short stories drawn from the author's vast treasure trove of experiences. He spent a lifetime in aviation, both military and civilian, became involved in the Cold War in Europe, nuclear testing at Christmas Island, topdressing in New Zealand, and spent many years flying the Pacific. Now retired, he has turned his hand to writing. His aviation background is reflected in many of these stories.

Set in Europe, North Africa, Hong Kong, New Zealand. Sydney, Honolulu, Christmas Island, Tahiti, Mo'orea, Rangiroa, and Bora Bora, it's a diverse and entertaining collection of fact and fiction, all based on the author's real-life experiences.

The dramatic engine failure described in *A Close Call In Tahiti* did occur, July 17th 1980, at Faa'a Airport in Papeete. The *Gun Running* happened back in 1957.

The author flew into Hong Kong's old Kai Tak airport many times. *Remember Kai Tak* describes just what it was like flying into that extraordinary place. The yacht featured in *Andria* is the *Jardilinka*, a well-known vessel in Hong Kong waters. The author was lucky enough to enjoy many cruises on this fine old vessel.

The Jury is a true story as are *A Curious Business, The Bottle*, and *Christmas Island. A Labs Attack* describes some of the things that went on during the Cold War, all true, these things happened.

Aerial topdressing features in *The Greening Of Northland,* an insight into this unique New Zealand industry.

I'm sure you'll enjoy reading these stories just as much as the author enjoyed writing them.

Travel Bites

'You're under arrest sir.'

'Excuse me?'

'You're under arrest.'

Excuse me indeed; how can this be? I was at the immigration desk at Los Angeles airport, just got off a big jet after flying all the way from Auckland, when I was confronted with this. *I was the Captain!*

A collection of short stories, all travel related. The author spent much of his life travelling the world, and accumulated a mother lode of experiences. Some of these are shared in this book.